LARAMIE LOVERS

Spur dropped off the branch and crouched behind the tree. The Circle S. At least he knew who they were. Someone crashed brush behind and to his left. Spur froze against the tree knowing that a moving figure is easy to distinguish in brush.

The sound came again and he saw movement. Automatically, Spur lifted the Spencer and sent three rounds into the brush where he saw the motion.

A scream, then cursing followed quickly. All was quiet for a few moments. Then a piercing bellow of pain.

"Come help me, you bastards! He done shot me bad. Gut shot me. Come get me out of here."

SPUR #25

LARAMIE LOVERS

DIRK FLETCHER

LEISURE BOOKS NEW YORK CITY

A LEISURE BOOK®

June 2005

Published by

Dorchester Publishing Co., Inc.
200 Madison Avenue
New York, NY 10016

ISBN 0-8439-2597-3

The name "Leisure Books" and the stylized "L" with design are trademarks of Dorchester Publishing Co., Inc.

Printed in the United States of America.

Visit us on the web at www.dorchesterpub.com.

LARAMIE LOVERS

1

The snarling, deadly sound of the heavy rifle shot blasted into Spur McCoy's consciousness at almost the same fraction of a second that a whispering lead bullet ripped through the warm Wyoming air not a foot from his head.

Spur dove off his roan gelding, hit the hard ground on his hands and left shoulder, and rolled behind a boulder big enough to protect him for the moment. His horse pranced a few nervous steps away, then stopped to nibble on some early spring grass.

McCoy huddled behind the rock waiting for the attack to continue. He had no idea who was gunning for him. He had arrived in Laramie late the night before on the Southern Pacific train, found a room at the little village's only hotel and dropped onto the hard bed exhausted.

This morning he had rented the roan for a look-around the area before he settled down to dig into the reason he came to Laramie.

Now the priorities had changed. Number one now was staying alive.

A voice came from a scattering of higher rocks to his left. "What the hell you doing riding in here, stranger?"

"He's trying to get hisself kilt, that's what he's doing!" a second, younger voice brayed with an answer.

"Naw, he's just plain shit dumb, that's all. Bet I can wing him 'fore he runs ten yards." It was a third voice that sounded heavier, older.

Spur had only his pistol. He had borrowed a Spencer rifle that morning from the livery man, not really expecting to need one so quickly. Now the repeating weapon nestled in the saddle boot on the horse five yards away.

Spur McCoy was six-two and in fighting trim at a hundred and ninety-five pounds of solid muscle and bone. He was thirty-two years old, top agent for the U.S. Government's Secret Service, and responsible for all the states and territories west of the Mississippi river.

"Hell, he ain't gonna try to run!" a new voice called from the same general area.

"Bet I can encourage him," the younger voice shrilled. A rifle shot slammed into the silence of the Wyoming high prairie. The round caught the roan in the head and she went down with a scream of protest. The beast rolled half over, then shrilled a scream again and died.

"We coulda sold that animal, you bastard!" a voice screeched.

"Don't fret about it, Blade. You get the saddle."

Blade, Spur would remember the name. He lay there trying to figure it out. Four or five men in good positions. Whoever fired at him the first time had missed on purpose. Nobody toting a rifle in Wyoming would miss at thirty yards unless he wanted to.

Why? Spur gave up trying to figure it out. The big question was how could he get out of here without a dozen holes in his hide? In front there was no chance. Behind him was another boulder, then a few more. He might make it to the rim of broad-leafed cottonwood in the low spot. Once there he could at least defend himself. With a pistol?

First the rifle. The roan had rolled toward him. That would help a yard or two. When she went down the Spencer had fallen out of the boot and slid toward him. It was still ten feet away. He made up his mind at once. Surprise.

Spur bunched his powerful legs under him, then in one swift move he surged away from the rock in a bent-over position, took three strides, grabbed the Spencer and dove for the bulk of the roan for protection.

Two rifle rounds needled through the air around him as he dove. One more slapped into the dead body of the saddle horse. Spur was untouched so far. Now all he had to do was get back.

He levered a round into the Spencer, a dandy 7-shot repeating rifle that had been his favorite for years. He peered over the horse a second, then dropped down. Best spot for a bushwhacking was the rocks dead ahead. He'd give them some return fire.

Spur pushed the Spencer muzzle over the roan and cranked off a round, then surged to his feet, fired again, dove and rolled toward the rock.

A rifle round slammed into the heel of his boot and tore the heavy leather buildup half way off. Two more shots missed. Then he was behind his rock again.

He studied the enemy around the far end of the boulder. He had been lucky so far. Down there were three notches which formed perfect firing spots. He bent around the rock and pounded two shots into the slots of the rock, heard a shouted curse, then he pulled back.

A dozen rifle rounds shattered on the granite boulder. Spur grinned. He'd made them mad. As soon as the surge of firing was over, he judged the distance to the next safe cover. Twelve, maybe fifteen feet. Four good running steps—if he had time and was lucky.

He had no choice. To stay where he was would invite circling by one or two of the bushwhackers. They would have an open shot and for him it would be sudden death.

Spur fired once more at the enemy, mindful of his ammunition supply. As he often did, he had shaken out twenty rounds for the Spencer from the box he got from the livery and put them in his jacket pocket. Still, that was damn few.

He jolted away from the rock without thinking about it. Spur darted one way, then cut back and dove for the safety of the next boulder big enough for cover. He felt the slug tear into his upper leg but before it hurt, he was behind the rock and safe.

He pulled up his left leg and saw the blood. There were two holes in his jeans. The round had slashed through two inches of his leg, missing the bone. He'd have to care for it later. He could hear the men behind the rocks talking. Now and then a round came his way to keep him honest.

From here his route to the trees was easier. The next rock was only six feet away, then he had cover the rest of the way. Without giving them a lot of time to plan anything, he jumped to the cover of the next bigger rock. A round hit the granite but too late to find any flesh.

From there Spur bent over and ran into the screening trees. The cottonwood was sturdy and big, gaining its life's water from the now dry creek that must run full in spring thaw.

Spur was about five miles north of town. He could use a horse but it was't necessary. He had more need to return some angry lead against the bushwhackers. Also, he wanted to know who they were and why they attacked a stranger without warning.

McCoy had come to Laramie to talk to the sheriff about a problem he had with a big rancher who had vanished two months ago. That job would have to wait.

It was still morning, the sun was warm, but not overly hot. He worked forward, downstream on the dry creek bed. He kept out of sight of the rocks where the shooters were. Spur had learned to move through brush from the Indians. He never took a step without making sure his weight would not break a dry stick or rustle a leaf.

Fifty feet down the stream bed he came to a larger broad leafed cottonwood. By standing on the first low crotch he could see the back side of the rocks that were his objective. Two men remained there, rifles over the top, waiting.

Spur wanted to gun down the two men, but he knew he couldn't, even if they had shot at him first. He leveled the Spencer in on the pair. First he had reloaded the tube so he had eight shots, seven in the tube and one in the chamber. Then he called, knowing his voice would distort through the trees and make his location hard to figure.

"Why did you men shoot at me?"

The two on the rocks looked around. Before he could react three rifles from another location fired toward him. They had no target but figured on the tree. One round came close, chipping wood beside him.

The two men he could see pointed at him and turned. Spur fired. The first man screamed and slammed backwards off the rock.

The second man scurried behind the rock.

"Bastard!" he bellowed. "You done kilt poor old Ned! Now you get it for certain. We was just funnin' with you. Now we show you what Circle S riders do to trespassers and bastards who gun down our riders!''

Spur dropped off the crotch and crouched behind the tree. The Circle S. At least he knew who they were. Someone crashed brush behind and to his left. Spur froze against the tree knowing that a moving figure is easy to distinguish in brush. However, a target that remains motionless is ten times as hard to find. Like a pheasant that crouches down when threatened and will fly only when kicked out of the hiding spot.

The sound came again and he saw movement. Automatically, Spur lifted the Spencer and sent three rounds into the light brush where he saw the motion.

A scream, then cursing followed quickly. All was quiet for a few moments. Then a piercing bellow of pain.

"Come help me, you bastards! He done shot me bad. Gut shot me. Come get me out of here.''

A voice came from the rocks again.

"Dreek, you know better'n that. Rules say every man for hisself. Rules say no prisoners. Hell, you remember that.''

"Yeah, Dreek, you got yourself shot. You get back to the ranch. I ain't about to come under his gun. Who is that guy, anyway?''

"Fuckers! You can't leave me here! All I need is my horse. Bring me my horse, damn you!''

"The old wheel spins around and around, Dreek. Just wasn't your turn to win. We're getting out of here. Seems I remember asking you for some help about six months ago, over in Kansas. Remember, Dreek? Hell, you didn't even answer me.''

A pistol fired four times. None of the rounds were aimed at Spur.

"Bastards! Fucking bastards!''

The small stretch of woods was quiet for a few

minutes. Then Spur heard leather squeak, and
horses move away.

"Bastards!"

Spur moved up slowly on the man they called
Dreek. He still had at least his pistol.

It took McCoy twenty minutes moving cautiously
through the growth to get to the man. By then
Dreek was so weak he couldn't hold up his gun. Spur
sat down beside the bushwhacker, pushed away his
six-gun and looked at the wound. One of the rifle
rounds had hit Dreek in the gut and come out his
back. He was bleeding to death inside and outside.

Dreek was about forty, with a beard. He wasn't a
big man. He snorted when he saw Spur.

"You my damn executioner?"

"Looks like it. What was this all about?"

"You're on Circle S land. We was just having
some sport with you."

"A strange kind of entertainment."

"Hell, it was all in fun, until you got that rifle and
splattered some lead into Willy. He got damn mad."

"You men riders for the Circle S?"

"Oh, hell yes. We're riders." Dreek tried to laugh,
but spit up blood. He shook his head. "Damn, not
long now."

"Tell me about the Circle S. What happened out
there?"

"Happened? Not much. Just a ranch. Gonna sell
off the steers, get our payroll up again. Kind of slack
for a while there. Especially in Sixty-Seven and
Sixty-Eight."

Spur frowned. "I don't understand. What was bad
about those two years?"

Dreek laughed softly. His color was bad, too much
blood was draining from his veins.

"Hell, we all went our own ways. Then we got
Cameron back. He told us he could make it like old

times, the good times. Hell yes, he did, too. Last few years . . . great!''

Dreek coughed then. Blood spewed out of his mouth gushing over his shirt and pants in a red froth.

"Like old times? I don't understand. Are you talking about an outlaw band? I've never heard of a Cameron who's wanted.''

"Damn right!" Dreek said. "Never will." He shook his head. "Nobody never will.''

Dreek grinned at Spur, blood surged out of his mouth again and he fell back against the small tree never to take another breath.

Spur searched the man for some papers, but found only a pocket knife, a plug of chewing tobacco, and two double eagles in a small purse. He left it all there. His friends would come back for his body.

Spur took time out and checked his leg again. Most of the bleeding had stopped where the rifle round had lanced through the back of his left thigh. He pulled down his pants, cut the tail off the blue shirt and made an effective bandage with the shirt strips and his neckerchief. Then he pulled up his pants and started hunting a horse to ride.

Spur found Dreek's mount after a fifteen minute search. It was a big black, a fine animal and easy to identify. It even had a new looking Circle S brand on its left hip. The black munched on the shoots of grass and snorted when Spur took the reins.

"Easy, boy . . . easy does it. You'll be getting a new rider now. Just settle down.''

Spur's easy way of talking and his confident tone calmed the big animal. McCoy had been good with animals since his first pet puppy in the New York town house. He hefted the Spencer rifle and lifted into the saddle.

It was western style, a little shorter than Spur liked but easy enough to sit. The ride back to town seemed shorter, but still he kept watching over his shoulder. There was no pursuit. He made up his mind about the big black well before he came to the livery.

He would turn the mount in. He would be found and recognized by men from the Circle S. At least that way Spur could isolate the killers who had come after him. It might be a place to start.

At the big barn on the edge of town, he turned the horse in, gave his name and said he'd ridden out that morning. There was a different wrangler on duty and he accepted the animal, then scowled.

"Don't never remember seeing a mount that good around this place. Old man Dowd must have spent some money."

Spur left the livery and went on down the street. As he walked he was aware of the pain in his left leg. He'd have to get it checked, but not before he talked to the sheriff.

Laramie couldn't be called a town yet. Three years ago there was nothing on the spot except an Overland stage swing station and what had once been a Pony Express stop back in 1862.

The railroad had changed all of that. When the mighty Union Pacific came blasting into the area, it brought with it a whole menagerie of camp followers, fast buck sharpies, prostitutes and gamblers.

The surveyors went through first and hardly ruffled the landscape. Then the engineers came to form up the grade and somewhere behind them were the track layers.

"Hell on Wheels" was what the railroad construction camps were often called. These mushrooming communities sprang up every few miles as the railroad moved along, ever westward. Often they died as soon as the rails moved ten miles away and a new site was picked up for the next tent city.

Spur could remember some of them; North Platte, Julesburg, Cheyenne, Laramie and Corinne. They began with a big tent that some enterprising merchant-gambler put up. The tents were stocked with the cheapest whiskey available, the best prostitutes they could wrangle into coming along, and cards and wheels of chance.

As many as four-hundred rust-eaters worked the railhead with the "perpetual train" that pushed a long flatcar to the very end of the tracks to make it easier for workers to get rails, tools, ties and use the rolling blacksmith shop.

The four hundred men lived in 85-foot long boxcars with bunks slung three or four high. They worked hard and played, gambled and whored just as hard. Most quickly lost their thirty-five dollars a month in wages before the tent stakes were firmly in place.

Spur had watched one of the rail head tent cities when it was roaring back in Sixty-Eight. There had been gamblers, saloonkeepers, pimps, whores, con men and every other shade of fast buck man in the West. The whores walked around the camp with derringers strapped to their waists. He'd heard they were deadly accurate with the close-in weapons.

The code of Western chivalry toward women prevented anyone from taking action against the prostitutes even when they robbed and shot up the men they serviced.

Now, almost three years after the tracks went through, Laramie was still here. It had not faded away with the camp followers. Fifteen or twenty frame buildings made up the business section of town. Maybe forty or forty-five small houses completed the settlement. Beef and the stock yards were almost the only reason that Laramie had survived.

It was a start. In another ten years Laramie would

be ten times as big . . . or would have faded into history.

Spur had dressed in worn jeans, an old blue shirt and a lightweight black vest when he had left on his ride that morning. He wanted to melt into the landscape as a cowboy.

Now he fit right in as he walked down the short main street. The sheriff's office was in the small frame building that boasted it was the court house for Albany county.

Somebody told him there were only four counties in all of Wyoming. That made it easier to get organized for territorial status. As the population grew, new counties would be carved out of the four.

Sheriff Stan Dryer looked up from his desk in back of a low railing that separated the outer section of the office from the inside.

"I'm hunting the sheriff," Spur said.

"Found him," Dryer said. "Business?"

"For damn sure, Sheriff. Can we talk private?"

Sheriff Dryer nodded and waved Spur into a small office to one side.

"Usually, I'm in here," Dryer said. He settled in a rocking chair behind a small desk and rubbed his chin that had a day's growth of stubble on it. At least half of the bristles were white.

Spur closed the door and sat in the chair across the inexpensive desk.

The sheriff held out his hand. "Name's Dryer, like it says on the sign." Spur took the hand.

"McCoy, Spur McCoy is my name." He took out his wallet, removed a tintype and unfolded a piece of paper stuck to the back of it.

"Sheriff, I'm a United States Federal Secret Service officer here on official business. That card grants me police powers in any of the states or territories, and instructs all law enforcement agencies to cooperate with me."

The sheriff took out a pair of spectacles, adjusted them on his nose and read the folded paper. He grunted.

"Never heard of no Secret Service before. But this sure looks like the genuine article." He handed the paper back. Spur folded it and pressed it against the tintype, then stuck a second thin metal picture to the back covering the identification.

"Sheriff Dryer, I want to keep my official capacity here a secret. I came in response to a message from the county clerk, I believe. Your name was mentioned."

"Yep. I told the clerk to write the letter. My hand ain't too steady since my fainting spell. Doc said it was a minor stroke. Anyway, it's all true, what Will told you in the letter. This big rancher's whole family and crew just vanished. Over night there was a new outfit running the place. Owner, boss, crew, the works."

"A big spread?"

"They claim about ten thousand acres, but must work over forty thousand with their stock. Out here property lines ain't what they are back East."

"The letter said something about a change of ownership being recorded by the county clerk." Spur said.

"Yep. That was first time anybody knew about the change. A gent by the name of Curt Cameron showed up with the grant deed signed over, and a bill of sale signed by the former owner. Receipt was for thirty-thousand dollars cash and a home in Illinois."

"Nobody in town saw the family or any of the crew after the sale?"

"Not a hide nor hair of them. The Circle S men used Laramie a lot while they was there. Can't fancy them just riding away without a by-your-leave."

"Does seem odd. What did this Cameron say?"

"Some wild story about old man Shuntington getting called back to Missouri where his people lived to take over a family business. He had to sell quick and ride for Cheyenne to catch the train."

"But the train runs right through Laramie," Spur said, interrupting. "Why would he ride an extra fifty miles?"

"Exactly what the clerk asked this Cameron. He just shrugged, and said Shuntington was a crazy old coot who might do anything."

"How old was he?"

"Ollie Shuntington was about forty-five. His wife was a couple of years younger. They had two kids but both were away at some kind of college or finishing school."

"Foreman? He still there?"

"Not far as I can tell," Sheriff Dryer said. "Looks like the whole crew got laid off and replaced." The lawman scratched his thinning hair. "Funny about that, too. This new owner didn't hire a single man from town. Always half a dozen hands looking for some riding work. Damn strange."

"How big is the usual crew out there?"

"Right now, before roundup? Probably about forty hands, give or take a handful."

"About right. Sheriff, I took a ride out that direction this morning. Got about four or five miles up the river and five or six riders bushwhacked me. Killed my horse, tried to kill me. Two of them wound up dead along the river."

"Damn! You don't say! Heard they could get mean about strangers riding their land."

"Two of them won't bother anyone again. You write up a report and I'll sign it. Line of duty."

Sheriff Dryer stared at Spur. His long face went slack and he sighed. " 'Fraid I can't even go check the bodies. Me and my one deputy got warned off the place.''

"You're the law in this county. You can go anywhere you want to.''

"If I want to get shot. I ain't as young or as good
with weapons as you must be. The Circle S will take
care of the burying themselves. Happened once
before, two weeks ago.''

"And you let them get away with it?''

"Damn right. Cameron's got an army out there. I
don't. That's why I sent a letter for you.''

Spur walked over to the window and looked out at
the side street. "What do you think happened to the
Shuntingtons?''

"Both must have been killed. I knew them. Good
church people, every Sunday morning. Belinda
wouldn't miss church for any reason. They're both
dead all right. The big puzzle is I just can't figure
out what happened to a crew of forty cowboys.''

Spur scowled at the lawman, then a shiver
straightened him up in the chair.

"You suggesting there might be forty more bodies
out on that ranch?''

"I hope to God there ain't.''

"What we need now is some evidence. No chance
now that I can sign on as a hand out there. I want to
stay unofficial here. I'll be able to find out more that
way. Remember, I'm just another out of work cowhand.''

The sheriff nodded and Spur walked out the door
and down the boardwalk. His first stop would be the
doctor's office he had seen last night on the way to
the hotel. Was it down this way, or back the other?
He wasn't sure.

The little town was wide open and roaring. A
pistol snarled behind him. Spur heard the round
shatter a window in the saloon beside him and he
darted into the nearby alley mouth. Who the hell
was shooting at him this time?

2

Spur hit the shiplap side of the bar five feet down the alley and worked his way back toward the boardwalk. As he came to the corner he dropped to a crouch. Just at that moment a pistol fired from the other direction down the street. The round slammed into the shiplap splintering off a piece.

Two gunmen!

Spur spun, his Colt .44 snapping around to a new target. The man was a cowboy. As if in slow motion, Spur saw the man's big six-gun moving down to aim at his new position. The rider was in his late thirties, bearded, a dark brown hat and a tan leather vest.

Spur fired once, saw the bullet jolt into the man's chest, then he turned and looked for the second man across the street. A figure near a vanishing puff of blue smoke faded into a half dozen people around a saloon.

The secret agent watched the scene, glanced back at the first attacker. He was down on the boardwalk, his six-gun three feet from his extended hand. He wasn't moving. Spur turned and looked for the second bushwhacker across the way.

One man broke free of the others and charged across the street, a gun in each hand. He fired as he ran. Spur ducked as the first round chipped raw wood over his head. He edged lower, saw the gunman grab a horseman riding by and used the horse as a shield walking the mount closer and closer to the alley mouth.

No chance to hit the attacker, and big odds that he would wound the rider or mount if he fired.

Spur saw he was shielded from the gunman's view. He stepped around the corner and ran down the boardwalk past the saloon and darted into the next store.

Too late he saw it was a seamstress, with fancy women's goods and clothes on racks and two dress forms with garments being made on them.

"Sorry, ma'am, gent out there is trying to kill me," Spur said to a blur of a woman sitting at a sewing machine.

He slid to the floor near the door and peered out the glass panel. The bushwhacker had left the horse and stared at the empty alley. The man swore, ran into the mouth of the opening, then came out, his gun still ready.

He looked at the drinking den's open door beside the alley, swore again, angled across the street and vanished into the Tumbleweed Saloon.

"Was that man in the white hat the one who shot at you?"

Spur turned and for the first time looked at the woman sitting behind a sewing table. She was about thirty, he estimated, a little heavy with a pretty face and sharp, penetrating eyes.

"Yes, ma'am, that's him. Know who he is?"

"I thought you might. He's a stranger so that probably means he's one of the riders from the Circle S ranch outside of town." She hesitated and her eyes softened as she watched him. "You're new in town as well, aren't you?"

"Train, last night. So far I've been shot at by two different groups. This is not a friendly place."

"Oh, but it is!" she burst out quickly. Then she laughed. "I mean, I like Laramie. It's going to be a fine little city some day."

"Let's hope so. Pardon my manners. My name is Spur McCoy."

She smiled and a touch of a blush colored her neck.

"Pleased to meet you. I'm Amy York. I don't imagine you need any dresses made."

Spur laughed. "Afraid not. But I thank you for letting me hide from that killer over there."

"I heard the shots." She shook her head in dismay. "I just don't understand you men and your guns."

"Way it's supposed to be, Miss York. I certainly don't understand hemstitching or blind button-holes."

She nodded. One hand twisted a strand of her long brown hair. Amy looked up at him once, then quickly away. Spur waited, smiling.

"Mr. McCoy, would you . . . that is . . . I mean, it's almost noon. Would you like to have a bite to eat with me?" She stormed ahead quickly so she wouldn't stop and run. "I live in back and I have some fresh fruit that came in on the train, and I'd make you a sandwich or whatever."

She closed her eyes and lowered her head. "Goodness! I don't know when I've been so forward!" She glanced up at him warily. "I'm sorry, Mr. McCoy. It was rude of me to ask. You really don't have to answer at all. I'm sorry."

"Amy, I'd love to have lunch with you. I'll know for sure that nobody is going to shoot me, right? And I want to ask you some questions."

"You will?" Amy's eyes widened. "Oh, my goodness! My kitchen isn't cleaned up at all! I'll need at least a half hour! Could you wait here? Oh, no. My goodness!"

Spur walked over to where she still sat.

"Miss York, there's no cause to fuss. I'm just common people, and you're doing me a favor. Besides, it's not every day I have a chance to eat with a pretty lady."

Amy looked up, some of her shyness gone. She watched him a minute, then smiled. "Mr. McCoy, that's the nicest thing anyone has said to me for a long time. Since the last time I saw Mr. and Mrs. Shuntington, I guess."

She went to the front of the small shop, locked the door and pulled a shade down over the glass. Many such window shades on businesses had been hand lettered like this one on the outside to say, "Closed."

Amy smiled again. "Right back this way, Mr. McCoy. And welcome to my humble home, such as it is."

Spur had noted her remark about the Shuntingtons. She might have made a dress for the woman. He would probe it later.

The rear of the shop had been made into a small apartment. There was a living room, tiny kitchen and what looked like two bedrooms opening off the main room.

"This is it," she said. "It suits me fine and with no more business than I do, it certainly is all I can afford." She led him into the kitchen and pointed to a chair.

"Sit down and read the weekly newspaper from Cheyenne. I don't know why I take it. Cheyenne is a long ways off and I don't get any business from there."

The meal was delicious. She made roast beef sandwiches for them, thin slicing a roast she said she had cooked last night and kept in her ice box.

"Yes, of course I have an ice box. It's just a home made affair, but ice is inexpensive here, and I can keep milk and meat fresh for four or five days without it spoiling. A friend made the ice box for me. We have plenty of ice here in the winter and the men cut it out of a pond from the river and put it in our town ice house, packing it down with straw. It lasts most of the summer, at least through August. Then the weather starts to get cold again."

Spur took a bite of the sandwich. She had found some lettuce, used a home made mayonnaise, and even put on a dill pickle.

"Sorry, I don't usually run on at the mouth that way."

"The sandwich is wonderful. You could start up a small cafe on the side."

She blushed lightly and looked down at her own sandwich. They had coffee and some of the fruit for dessert. When they finished they stood and she hesitated.

"Thanks for the meal, it was really good. Oh, you mentioned the Shuntingtons. Did you work for them?"

"Yes, I made three dresses for the Mrs. She was a wonderful lady."

"Did she say anything about leaving town, selling their big ranch?"

Amy shook her head, her face worked for a moment but she beat back sudden tears.

"No! not a word. That's why I'm afraid . . . why I'm afraid something bad happened to them."

"Were you working on a dress for her when they left?"

"Yes! It was almost done. I still have it. She had been in town a week before for a final fitting. She said she'd be in to pick it up the next Saturday when the men came to town. She even paid me for it in advance. What a nice lady."

"Good, Miss York. You've helped me." He turned toward the door into the store.

"Oh, Mr. McCoy. There is something else. A small

problem maybe you could help me with."

"Of course, you've been the one helping me all morning."

"Good. It's in the other room." She led the way through a door that opened into a bedroom. Amy turned and faced him, her features alive, flushed. She gripped his vest and pulled his head down and kissed his lips. She held the kiss a long time, then her tongue probed his lips. At last she released him.

"Mr. McCoy, I used to be married. My man died in the big war. I loved him dearly. But he's gone. I—" she blushed again, then stormed ahead. "I ain't had a man for five years, Mr. McCoy. I wondered if you might do me good and proper right now."

"Miss York—"

"Don't say no, right off. Let it simmer a minute." She kissed him again, her breasts pressed hard against his chest, her hips pushed against his crotch and she began a slow grinding. His mouth came open this time and she probed inside.

When she let go of him her hands tore open the buttons down her dress front. She pushed the bodice open and lifted her chemise so one large breast showed.

"I'd be ever so grateful, Mr. McCoy. No demands, no strings, just a good bedding so I don't close up into a virgin again. I really need your loving!"

Before he could react, she pushed the dress off her shoulders and lifted the pink chemise over her head. Her breasts hung heavy, with large pink areolas and small, intensely red nipples that stood tall now with warm blood.

"Amy, I don't want to take advantage of you. Is this really and truly what you want to do?"

As he asked, she pulled the dress off over her head and wiggled out of some fancy new style drawers with elastic in the waist. She stood in front of him naked, her arms out.

"Mr. McCoy, for five years I've been waiting for you to come into my shop. Yes, it's what I really and truly want to do. Please, right now and for the rest of the day!"

"Amy, there's no argument in the world like a beautiful lady standing naked in front of me. Not a chance you can lose that contest."

She smiled and stepped up to him, catching both his hands and putting them over her breasts. She leaned in close and whispered. "Spur McCoy, I need you to fuck me good about six times!"

He chuckled. "Six? I'm not seventeen anymore. But we sure as hell can give it a good try!"

Spur picked her up and carried her to the bed, put her down softly, and kissed her lips.

"I want to . . . Spur, can I? Let me undress you!"

She did, first his boots and socks, then his vest and slowly his shirt. It was as if this were a happening of great consequence and she wanted to be able to remember it for years.

When she had his clothes off she frowned at the makeshift bandage and checked his leg. "You've been shot!" At once she ran to the kitchen and brought back dressing and salve and alcohol. She went to work cleaning the two wounds, treating the punctures and bandaging his leg skillfully. "That should hold you for a day or two." He thanked her with a kiss.

Spur fondled her breasts. They were heavy and he could feel blood pulsating through her growing nipples.

"Spur, lover, do me quick the first time. Been so . . . so long. Put it inside me right now. I'm ready, lord knows I've been ready for five years!"

Amy turned on her back and spread her legs and lifted her knees. She was ready, Spur decided as his lance slid into her sheath with almost no resistance.

"Wonderful!" Amy whispered. Then she shrieked

and her whole body trembled and vibrated. She shrieked again and again as a climax slammed its way through her entire body. She whimpered at the last and her eyes came open. Spur would never forget the smile on her face.

"Oh, goodness! Five years! I tried to do it by myself, lots of times, but just never works. Oh, goodness!"

Spur began to stroke into her and at once Amy climaxed again. This time Spur went with her and blasted his own satisfaction deep into her sheath as she faded on her second climax.

When she opened her eyes this time, Spur had recovered and lay over her resting.

"Tell me about Spur McCoy," Amy said. "Where do you come from? What are you doing in Laramie?"

"Not a lot to tell. I grew up in New York City where my father has three or four stores. I went to school there and then on to college. When I graduated I worked in dad's businesses for a couple of years, then joined the army as a second lieutenant."

"You were in the war then. My Ned was killed at Bull Run."

"I was in the infantry. Served for two years and came out a Captain. Then I went to Washington D.C. where I was asked by an old family friend to be a military liaison for the United States senator from New York. I was with him until just after the war ended."

"Land sakes! You're a celebrity. Worked in the U.S. Senate with a senator, and a war hero and all."

"Not much of a hero. I survived. I think all of the heroes were the men like your husband who died. I was lucky." He looked around.

"Amy, would you have anything to drink in the place?"

"Brandy!" she said. "Yes, I got some for cooking, but never used much. Yes, some brandy."

As she left the bed and hurried out into the kitchen it was more obvious that Amy was more than a little heavy, but she was good in bed. Spur tried to remember any of the women he had made love to who were not good in bed. Yes, there had been one or two, but it was only because they had worked at not enjoying it and had not let him enjoy it either. But they were few and with many states between them.

Amy came back with the bottle of brandy and two water glasses. She poured and they toasted.

"To your health, and to a good man in your life soon," Spur said.

Amy blinked back a tear and nodded. "That would make me truly happy. Almost as happy as I am right now, standing here naked in front of a man I met only an hour ago, still glowing with the delight of making love, and expecting a lot more. I'm just glad as all get out that you ran into my store."

"So am I, Amy. This is excellent brandy."

While he was getting his strength back he probed about the Shuntingtons. "Do you remember Mrs. Shuntington saying anything at all about selling the ranch? Was she the kind of person who would tell you if anything important was coming up?"

Amy put her chin in her palm, her forearm flattening her breast. "Nope, Mrs. Shuntington never said a single word about moving, about selling the ranch, about anything out of the ordinary happening. I've been making dresses for her for almost four years now, and we were good friends. She and I talked about just about everything, even about bedding our men.

"We were good friends. She'd come in once or twice a week sometimes, just to talk. I'm dead sure,

Spur, that she didn't know nothing about moving or selling the ranch."

She watched him a moment. "Spur, you from some insurance company, or a private detective like them Pinkertons, and you come here to find out what happened to the Shuntingtons?"

"Something like that, Amy, but you can't tell anyone. I'm supposed to be just another out of work cowhand."

Amy grinned. "I like knowing a secret about you. Makes me feel all warm and good inside." She giggled. "Course, just getting fucked better than I ever been done in my whole life might have something to do with it, too. Do me again, good fucker! Do me again before I start begging you!"

She jumped on the bed and Spur was close behind. This time he rolled her over and put her on top.

"Really? Will it work this way? I mean, can we fit?" She giggled and saw that indeed it would work.

"Guess you know I never done it this way before."

"Figured that out," Spur said.

Then they both were lost in the lust of the moment and Amy quickly picked up the motion and before long was riding Spur like he was a stud horse.

"My goodness, I've never felt anything like this before," she said. Then her time came and she yelped and screeched and cried and wailed as the action brought her to another surging climax.

When the fury died Spur had reached his peak as well, and they clung together for ten minutes before rolling apart.

She pushed up on one elbow and stared down his long pale white and starkly brown form.

"Pretty Spur McCoy, why don't you just stay here in Laramie? I'll support you. Open that restaurant. We'll make a living and you can make love to me twice a day for the rest of our natural lives!"

"Twice a day and I'd be dead in six months!"

"All right, once a day so you can live two years. Best two years of your life."

Spur reached over and played with her breasts. "Tempting, but I'm afraid I better pass. I'm a fiddlefoot, never stay in one place very long. Got to keep moving. Not that you don't have everything it takes to keep a man happy. And you sure as hell know how to use it."

She giggled and blushed.

"Besides, my work moves me around. You couldn't trust me out on the job with all the pretty women I meet."

"With you, McCoy, I'd be willing to share. Just so you came back to my bed every couple of weeks."

"You have the rest of the afternoon to convince me. Hey, have you ever made love standing up?"

"Can't be done."

"Give me another ten minutes and I'll prove to you that it can be done."

It can. He proved it. Amy never did believe it.

3

Spur pulled on his clothes in the back room of Amy York's dress shop about three that afternoon. Amy hummed softly as she watched him. She sat on the bed grandly naked and teasing him with various suggestive poses.

"Now you be careful, Spur McCoy. The whole crew of fifty men from the Circle S is going to be gunning for you. I've seen it happen before here once. They hounded the blacksmith until he challenged one of them. As soon as he pulled out his gun, four of them shot him down without saying a word. Then they went to a saloon and bought drinks for everyone."

She scowled. "Spur, be careful and come back to me."

Spur hugged her tightly, kissed her lips and walked out the front door. He hurried directly to the sheriff's office where he gave a verbal report on the death of the cowboy in the street just before noon.

"Figured you in the fracas somewhere," Sheriff Dryer said putting on his spectacles to read a paper. "Had three witnesses who testified at least two men tried to gun you down. I got a report all made out. Just read it over and sign it. Both the bushwhackers were circle S riders, we're sure."

The sheriff looked at Spur, a frown growing on his face. "Just hope to hell this don't mean all fifty of them riders are going to storm into town and shoot up the place. We don't have that many guns in all of Laramie."

"I'll try to keep it on a more personal level than that, Sheriff Dryer. Soon as it gets dark, I'm going to pay a social call on the Circle S spread."

Dryer looked up, his thin face puzzled. "You gonna walk right into the damn lion's den when you know they'll shoot you on sight and then get nasty?"

"The lion will never know that I'm there, Sheriff. If someone spots me, I'll leave a calling card so they'll be sure. Without some direct information, we're stymied on this case. I simply need to see the lay of the land, investigate as much as I can as soon as I can."

Sheriff Dryer stoked his pipe "Damn glad it's you going out there to the Circle S and not me. Good luck."

Spur moved to the Johnson Dry Goods store and found the owner, Dick Johnson, a man who knew weapons and repaired them on the side. He sold new and used guns and repaired weapons of all kinds. Spur bought a used Spencer carbine the man had reworked.

Dick grinned. "Damn good piece. Wanted to keep it myself, but if you need it, welcome. Got to charge you seven dollars for it. But I'll throw in a box of fifty rounds. Damn fine weapon, that Spencer. Sometimes I wish it had more range, but hell, it's good for six hundred yards. I can't rightly see much further than that anyway."

Spur hefted the weapon. It measured 39-inches long overall, much shorter than the Spencer rifle that reached out to 47-inches. It used the same .52 caliber bullet and had the seven round magazine

that loaded through the butt of the stock. The thin
magazines could be carried in a small box holding
ten, giving a man 70 shots in a rush.

"Carbine's lots easier to use, if'n you riding a lot,"
the storekeeper said eyeing Spur's cowboy clothes.

"I tend to do that, yes," Spur commented. He
paid the man, bought another box of 50 rounds for
his Colt .44 six-gun and went out to the street.

He saw a group of four riders churn into town and
pull up at the Tumbleweed Saloon. They looked like
they could be from the Circle S, so Spur turned into
an alley off the main street and went the long way to
the livery. If he challenged a batch of Circle S riders
it would be on his terms and on his timing.

In ten minutes he had picked out a horse, bought
it for thirty dollars and paid another five for a used
saddle and halter.

"You the gent who rode in this morning with that
big black stallion, ain't you?"

"Might have been. Why?"

"Some Circle S riders came in here snorting fire.
Said somebody stole the horse from Dreek, one of
their riders. They pointed out the new brand and
just took him right out of the stable. Not even a
thank you."

Spur pulled a double eagle from his pocket and
flipped it to the livery man.

"Had a small misunderstanding with Dreek. He
shot my horse so I traded him for his, since he
wasn't going to be needing it anymore. No reason
you should take a loss on the mount you rented to
me."

The livery man grabbed the twenty dollar gold
piece and grinned.

"Now, that's right neighborly of you, friend. I
thank you. No way to reason with this new batch of
Circle S riders. Just no way a'tall."

Spur rode out of town to the south so he wouldn't

have to move down the Laramie main street. Someone had put up a sign and called it First Street. He
curved across the Union Pacific tracks, rode out of
town, and soon hit the Laramie river to the west. He
forded the river at the shallowest point he could
find, got his legs wet and then rode north beyond the
trees and out of sight of the town.

But he didn't go far. He stopped in some thick
brush of young cottonwood and box elder along the
stream and moved into the thicket until he couldn't
be seen. There he'd wait for darkness.

Spur ground tied the mount, a strong, steady
looking gelding about five years old that had a
pretty roan coat. The dark red glistened in the
sunlight and Spur wished he had a curry comb and
brush to give the animal a grooming.

Instead he drank from a small side stream that
came into the Laramie river, then settled down
against a log and pulled his hat down over his eyes.
He didn't expect any visitors and he would be alert
to anyone riding by on the trail north.

Since he was going on a night patrol, some shut-
eye now would come in handy. Spur relaxed and in a
few moments, he slept.

He roused to the chatter of a squirrel who was
surprised to find a human in his favorite hunting
ground. Spur pushed up his hat and looked around.
It was approaching dusk. He made sure his horse
had all he wanted to drink, then mounted and took
the trail north.

He had learned his lesson and would swing off the
track and move north parallel to the stream which
he discovered he was moving along downstream. It
grew larger the farther north he rode. Evidently it
emptied into the North Platte river, which then ran
south into the Platte in Nebraska, then on to the
Iowa line and into the mighty Missouri.

His left thigh hurt some, but not as much as he

had expected. The rifle round had punched through
in an instant without distorting much, leaving a
clean exit wound. Amy had done a good job
bandaging and treating it. Tomorrow he'd go see the
local sawbones and have him take a look at it. Right
now it didn't slow him up a bit.

It was soon dark, and there was no moon that
night, so Spur rode slowly, working his way north.
At one point he heard some singing and laughing,
saw a campfire, and skirted it by another quarter
mile. It sounded like the Circle S guards were
having a small party instead of tending to business.
For a moment the sound and the situation reminded
him of off duty soldiers. But these riders were certainly not soldiers and out here they should be
acting as lookouts, doing their job.

Another three miles along the Laramie river, he
topped a small rise and looked across the high
plateau and saw lights. He moved ahead slowly,
testing the lay of the land, watching for any
campfires, any sounds that could reveal a ring of
guards set out. There might be none. The Circle S
riders were over confident. They felt their
reputation for violence protected them so no one
would try to slip in. He was counting on that
arrogance to help him.

By the time Spur had walked his mount within a
hundred yards of the first barn and corral of the
spread, he had not heard nor seen any guards. He
tied his roan's muzzle shut with his kerchief so he
would not horse-talk, and left him tied to a tough
small shrub.

Spur felt as though he were back in the war. He
had slipped up on a lot of farms and ranches and
patches of woods and draws and hillsides back then
only to find them come alive with Rebel forces.

Now he had no idea what kind of a force he faced.
Were they simply rabble gathered up to rustle a

whole ranch, cattle, crew, owner even the chuck
wagon cook? Or was it totally innocent, the result of
massive bad planning and bad luck on the former
owner's part?

He had to find out.

Spur slid to the ground twenty yards from the rear
of the nearest barn. He spotted a lookout after only
a few minutes of waiting. The man coughed, then
swore silently and lit a cigarette. A few moments
later the lonesome notes of a harmonica drifted from
the position.

"Red! You play another note and I'll cut your
guts out!" a voice called from somewhere near the
middle of the barnyard.

The harmonica music stopped.

Spur crept silently to his left around the musician
until he could edge into the far side of the barn.
Inside he found what he expected: a few stalls for
milk cows, several stalls for favorite horses, a mow
of cured hay with room for lots more. To one side sat
a feedbox with a lift top that held bins of feed grain.

It was a working ranch barn. Nothing unusual or
out of the ordinary—unless there were forty-five
bodies buried under the hay somewhere. That
simply could not have happened. He hoped. How
else did you get rid of a crew of men and the owners
and not leave a trace?

Spur climbed a ladder to the hayloft and watched
out the open haymow door. There was just enough
light to see across the barnyard. The main house
was forty yards away. A well stood in the middle of
the area with the gentle slope of the land running
downhill to the barns. A bunkhouse showed to the
left, now blazing with coal oil lamps.

He saw no other guards for a while, then spotted
one more with a rifle over his shoulder like a soldier,
walking around the main house. Was he protecting
someone inside, or keeping someone inside a

prisoner? The Shuntingtons could be held prisoner in there.

Maybe. No. Not logical. Why steal their ranch and let them live? No prisoners, that would be neater, smarter. And whoever worked a plan like this had to be smart.

A pair of men wandered out of the bunkhouse, lit ciarettes and came toward the barn. They stopped directly below Spur and talked. They had been in some kind of a discussion.

"Hell, I say we hang right here. Where we got to go? Besides, this is a good outfit. We get fed good, dry place to sleep every night, not one hell of a lot of work to do."

"Not much to do right now, that is. You ever done any roundup work or trail driving? When does Curt plan to ship the rest of these damn cattle?"

"Christ, but you are dumb, Doffler. We can't just ship them, got to be a buyer in Laramie to buy them first. You want to give away all your shares in this operation?"

"Naw, guess not." The man threw down his smoke and stamped it out. "Still, I like the old days better. Always something going on. Usual some woman around we could flip on her back."

"Them good old days is gone forever, Doffler. We take what we can get now, and this is a sweet deal."

"Better be."

The two walked back toward the bunkhouse.

Spur learned little by listening to the men. Obviously they were going to sell the cattle. But shares? What good old days were the men talking about?

Spur turned and looked around. His main interest now centered on the ranchhouse. He went down the ladder, slipped out of the barn and silently worked around the long way until he came up in back of the main house. Four rooms showed lights that he could see.

He lay in the weeds for ten minutes watching the house and the guard who circled it. The man came by every four minutes, regular as the Waterbury ticking in his pocket.

Spur waited unitl the guard made his pass behind the house, then Spur worked his way forward slowly on his belly, crawling within ten feet of the route the guard took. The man came again, but didn't even glance toward where Spur lay hidden in the high weeds. When the guard passed the edge of the house, Spur surged up in a run and charged to the lighted window on the ground floor twenty-feet away.

The shade was up. Spur looked inside. A woman stood in front of a bed and slowly took off her dress. She flung it aside, ground her hips and laughed at a man who sat on the bed. Spur couldn't hear what she said, but the wild squeal was plain enough to understand.

She ripped off clothes, throwing them one way and then the other. When she was naked she rushed at the man sitting on the bed, toppled him over and then sat on his face screaming in delight.

Spur hurried away from the window and back into the darkness just before the guard came around the house. The watchman paused and looked inside, then shook his head, rubbed his crotch and kept on marching around his post.

Spur lay in the brush trying to figure it out. He had used several military terms since he got on the ranch: post, marching, sentry. Why? As he thought it through, the whole place seemed to have a slightly out of focus military atmosphere. There was nothing concrete he could put his finger on to explain it.

Even with the military flavor, he had found

nothing to cause concern for the missing family. What if they had simply tired of the area, picked up and left without any notice? People probably did that every day in New York. Why not here?

The barn floor. It would be an ideal burial ground if you didn't want the bodies found. In a stall or an indoor corral for a half dozen horses, new dirt would not be evident. Nobody would think to look there for a body, or a pair of bodies—even forty-five corpses.

He took the same route into the barn as before, found a pitchfork and began pushing it into the ground floor everywhere he found the earth exposed. The stalls yielded only the acrid stench of ammonia from the urine. The three stiff tines of the fork dug into the soft ground an inch and stopped. Not here.

He tried the other spots, then went to the edge of the small corral built inside the barn. Again he found no soft spots around the sides. He was just ready to step through the doorway into the corral when someone jumped him from behind.

"What the hell you doing, stranger?" A voice screeched just as the body hit Spur. He had no time to grab for his six-gun. Instead he swung around, slammed the sturdy fork handle against the man's side, drew it back like a rifle with bayonette and rammed the three tines into the attacker's chest.

Only when the man blurted in pain and fell to his knees did Spur see the ten-inch knife he held. Another second or two and Spur would have been impaled on the big blade.

Spur watched the ranch hand's eyes go wide, then he bleeted in pain and toppled to one side. The man didn't have a chance in hell of living for ten minutes.

Spur worked his way to the same door he had used to get in before and cautiously stepped through it.

He heard a six-gun cocking, then a second one. His hand darted for his holster as he dove away from the sound, hit the dirt and rolled. His weapon was out as he came to his stomach, pushed up and raced into the blackness away from the barn.

Two guns blazed at him. The lead was wide. He darted in the opposite direction to confuse their sound-oriented target but kept pumping his legs. The two men behind him cursed and fired until their weapons were empty.

More lights bloomed in the ranch yard. A rifle spoke sharply and with authority but the bullet came nowhere near Spur. He ran steadily now, arms pumping, the Spencer Carbine in one hand.

Somewhere behind he heard horses calling to each other as men evidently saddled up. Someone shouted an order for six men to move out.

By then Spur found his roan, undid her muzzle and stepped on board. He rode away due south at a canter, waiting to see what the pursuit would be before he tested the speed of the big red. Chances were that some of the riders would come this way.

The sounds faded behind him.

Spur stopped and turned his ear toward the north. A light breeze stirred the grass on the plains, but he heard nothing. He resumed his ride, moving generally south, staying in the Laramie valley with the Medicine Bow Mountains to the south and west.

A half hour later he stabled the roan in the livery and walked up to the Medicine Bow Hotel where he had a room. It was on the second floor front. He picked up his key at the desk, noticed the strange look the night clerk gave him, then went up the stairs.

He had determined not to stay in his room that night. Too many people were interested in his where-abouts. He went down the hallway, paused at his door and then turned sharply as a door opened behind him. His hand lifted the Colt .44 from leather as he pivoted.

He saw only a large blonde woman who waved

him forward. She caught his arm and pulled him into her room, closing the door quietly. She held a finger over her lips.

"Your room ain't overly healthy for you tonight, Mister," she whispered. "I overheard two gents who were making a bet which one could kill you first. Later on I saw them in the lobby waiting for you to come back from wherever you went for a ride. Yep, they know about your horse and rifle, everything."

Spur saw the woman clearly now in the light of two coal oil lamps. She was taller than most women, probably five-six, with long wheat straw colored hair that came to her waist. She wore a robe over a full figure and stared at him now with a faint smile.

"You look like you're not used to getting rescued by a woman," she said with a soft laugh.

McCoy nodded. "True, especially one so beautiful."

"Save the blarney, you'll need it. From what I hear there are at least fifteen Circle S men in town wanting to punch holes all over your body with their six-guns slugs."

"People have tried that before," Spur said. "That's why I have no plans on taking advantage of your hospitality here in your room. Too dangerous for you."

"Take advantage?," she asked surprised. "Just how did you mean that?"

Before Spur could answer there was an explosion that blasted in the hallway, jolting the woman's locked door open. Spur looked through the inch-opening and saw his room directly across the hall had its door blasted off its hinges, hanging in splinters, and his room was filled with smoke and flames.

He closed the blonde woman's door gently.

"Maybe it would be a good idea if I stayed here for a while after all," he said.

"Timing," she said softly. "It's all in the timing."

4

Curt Cameron forked a load of scrambled eggs into his mouth and chewed quickly before he burst out laughing. Lucia had just finished serving him his breakfast and vanished for a moment. When she stepped back into the kitchen at the Circle S ranch house, she was as bare as she had been last night in the small bathtub.

"Ain't I a gorgeous, sexy pile of woman?" she said, throwing her chest out in a provocative pose. "Curt, you big cock, you better just finish eaten' up them eggs quick so you can start nibblin' on me in just any old place you want."

Curt had more eggs, then a bite of toast and home made jam, and a long drink of coffee.

"Lucia, you wild woman, what if the men look in the window?"

"None of them gonna see any part of me he probably ain't seen before, only then it was probably involved in some sexy action. Come on, Curt, I need a morning wake up poking."

"Woman, you tryin' to kill me off at an early age so you can get at my bank account? Twice a day is once too much for a man of my advanced years."

"You talk about money, honey. But you never showed me none. Just some figures in a little old

44

blue book about as big as a nickel."

"They call them bank passbooks, Lucia. But don't worry your pretty titties about that. You get dressed so I don't get all excited here and drop you right on the kitchen floor. You'd get splinters in your backside down there on the boards."

"Wouldn't mind," she said, thrusting her hips out in a series of three quick little bumps.

Curt swatted at her and she yelped and hurried out of the kitchen.

Curt had something more important to worry about this morning. One of the lookouts from last night was found dead, run through with a three tined pitchfork. Damn tough way to die. Curt scowled as he finished the coffee.

Who killed the man? More important, why? If it was a fight among the men, that was acceptable. Curt hoped it was an old grudge or a new one and a fair fight.

The alternative was what worried him. If there hadn't been a fight last night, it could mean they had an outsider snooping around, got himself caught and then turned the tables and killed the catcher. Damn, that really worried him. Things moving along smooth as Tennessee sippin' whiskey. Now this.

Lucia came back in, hugged him over the back of the chair and pushed her big breasts against his shoulders.

"Hey that feels good, my titties all snuggled up against you that way."

"Better, cause if you don't get the kitchen cleaned up I'm gonna have them ground up into sausages!"

She bit his ear lightly and went to the table.

Curt ambled outside to talk to his second-in-command, the foreman of the ranch.

Joel shook his head as he watched his boss. "Don't rightly reckon, Major. None of the men say they even heard an argument or scuffle last night. We got five or six guys in town looking for that skunk we missed yesterday. I'd say the killing happened by somebody from the outside."

"Got past our sentries?"

"Hell, a little old grandmother on a mule could do that. We ain't expecting any trouble. Said yourself we didn't have to have tight security around the ranch."

"Yeah, true. But now this." Curt kicked at the desert dry high plateau Wyoming dirt. It was a light sandy loam with lots of small rocks mixed in. "Get me Blade. I want him to see if he can find any tracks."

"He's in town looking for that skunk who killed Joe and Willy yesterday down by the breaks."

"Yeah, right. Get out the next best tracker we got and have him do a double circle about a hundred yards out, looking for any boot tracks or fresh horse prints from last night."

"Yes sir, you got it," Joel said and walked off toward the bunk house.

It was less than half an hour later when Joel and Curt knelt in the prairie south of the ranch house and stared at the tracks.

"Looks like the horse was ground tied or on this little brush. Critter was here some time considering the droppings. The boot tracks lead toward the ranch, and back toward the horse."

"Shit! We did have a visitor last night."

"Same one who rode onto the place yesterday?" Joel asked.

"Could have been. Find out in town everything you can about him. Who he is, what his name is, and why he's here snooping around."

"Maybe Blade will wipe him out first and we won't need to bother," Joel said.

"Maybe, but we have to make sure. Do it. Send

another man to town, now. One who can speak good
English without a heavy accent."

Joel nodded and ran for the bunkhouse.

Curt walked slowly back to the ranch house and
let the screen door slam as he went in.

Lucia meandered in drying her hair with a towel.
When she swung her long dark hair over her head
with the towel wrapped around it, he saw that she
was topless.

"You promised me St. Louis this Spring,
remember?" Lucia said. "When the hell we going to
St. Louis?"

"After you learn to wear clothes."

"I can wear clothes in the city. Let me show you.
You'll like St. Louis."

"I've been there before. I'm busting bigger
problems. We're needing to sell about five thousand
head of steers. That means getting them into a pen
somewhere. Most of these damn riders we have
never threw a rope in their lives."

"So hire some cowboys."

Curt snorted. "Oh, hell yes. And so much as admit
that we ain't what we say we are. Not a bloody
chance of my doing that. I might not be a college
graduate, but I know better than that."

Lucia flounced around, her breasts swinging.
"Never said I graduated, just that I went for a
while, 'cause this boy was going and I and him was
gonna get married."

"You thought you were, thought it with your
crotch. Get out of here."

Curt walked to the veranda and watched Joel
striding toward him.

"He gone?"

"Yeah, sent a good man, Walters. He's a great
talker, he'll find out who the polecat is."

"Anything else?"

"Yeah, Major. The boys are getting restless.

Nothing to do for too long. They get to thinking too much. Some of them say we still owe them a hundred dollars from that last job we did."

Curt looked up sharply. "You kept the company records, we owe anybody or don't we?"

"One or two, maybe six."

"So tell them after this score we'll settle up. We need to get two-thousand head of cattle in that lower pasture where we got that smooth wire fence across. Time we talk with Elliot Parker and find out how we sell these critters. When we have two-thousand rounded up and in that pen, we'll be ready. Take thirty men out and start moving them steers into the pen. Must have some cowboys in the bunch."

"Damn few, but we'll manage." Joel turned and walked smartly toward the bunk house. Curt called after him.

"When you get them on their way, come back. I've got another job for you."

Joel nodded. "Yes sir," he said.

Inside the ranch house, Curt found Lucia sprawled on the big bed combing her long dark hair. She had pulled off her blouse again and now sat up shaking her breasts at him.

"Just stay right where you are and get ready for a party," Curt said. He tossed her a pint bottle of whiskey.

"For me?" she asked.

"For you and Joel. He's due."

"No!" she shrieked. "I don't do that no more with them, just you. You promised me!" She screamed at him again.

"You hurt me!"

"Not half as bad as I'm gonna if you don't treat Joel right when he gets in here."

"You said I didn't have to service nobody but you no more! You promised me in Kansas!"

"So I changed my mind. He gonna use up your

pussy or something? Hell, you serviced half the damn company for the last two years. Why you bitching?''

"Because you said—"

She stopped when he drew back his hand.

"Things change. Getting harder to hold the company together. Six damn years we been a group now. That takes a lot of planning and a lot of work. You're part of it. Your part is to shut up your mouth and be nice to Joel. You act sexy and appreciate him. I'll be watching from the hall. You sex him up good and proper at least three times, or I'll wash your little pussy out with coal oil and you won't even piss for a week!''

Joel came back to the porch a few minutes later and knocked. Curt talked to him a minute, Joel grinned and walked into the living room, then cautiously down the hall to the bedroom. He left the door open a foot when he went inside.

Joel stood beside the bed. Lucia sat on it topless, frozen in place. When he looked at her, she smiled and shook her shoulders so her breasts bounced and swayed.

"My god but you're beautiful!" Joel said. He sat beside her and caught her breasts. "Look good enough to eat!" he said.

"Then eat them, Joel," she said. She reached for his shirt and began unbuttoning it.

From the hallway Curt watched a moment more. He waited until Joel had stripped off her skirt and dropped her on the bed. Joel kicked off his boots and rolled on top of her.

Curt walked down to the back of the house to what had been a laundry room. There was a single bed set up there. He locked the door behind him and looked at the bed.

On it sat a kid no more than seventeen. Curt had taken him on at the last ranch as an amusement.

The boy was naked, his stiff penis in his hand.

"You said to come after Joel got in the house," the boy said.

Curt nodded. Then a slow grin spread over his face. "Something different, son, a little change of pace. And I know that you like it.

"Anytime, anywhere, anyplace," the youth said. He left the bed and walked up to Curt and unbuckled his belt and began tugging down his pants.

Spur McCoy left the room across the hall from his blasted one about nine the next morning. The tall blonde lady's name was Etta, and she had been more than kind to share her bed with him, a poor soul under a vicious attack. He promised that he would see her again.

Now he viewed the remains of his former room. The door was still hanging on wounded hinges. He picked through the rubble, was glad it had not been a feather ticking or mattress, and soon found what was left of his suitcase. It had been under the bed and shielded from most of the blast. Still, it had six holes in it and the latch wouldn't work.

He picked up everything he owned, held the suitcase under his arm and walked slowly down the back steps to the alley. He peered around the doorway but saw nobody there.

After five minutes of working from alley to alley, he came to the Sheriff's office and slipped inside.

"Heard your room got dynamited last night," Sheriff Dryer said. "They know you're bad news for them." He tapped the dregs out of his pipe, scraped it and filled it with fresh tobacco but didn't light it. "Peers they don't want you to stay in town."

"Peers they don't. Care if I bunk in an empty jail cell tonight? You don't even have to lock the cell door."

The sheriff nodded and Spur put his suitcase in the cell nearest the door.

"Have some news for you," Sheriff Dryer said. "Morning train brought in a former resident, Rutger Shuntington. He's twenty-one, and has been in St. Louis going to school. I wired him when it was clear something was wrong, and he's just getting here. He's at the Medicine Bow Hotel."

"I better have a talk with him," Spur said. "How did you find out he came in?"

"He registered that way at the hotel and the room clerk sent me a message. He thinks it might be dangerous for the kid to be running around shouting his name."

"Agree. I'll go track him down, get him moved to an easier to defend room, maybe."

Spur found Rutger on the second floor. When he answered the knock on the door, he opened it wide at once.

Spur scowled.

"Rutger Shuntington, my name is Spur McCoy. I'm a United States law enforcement officer here to find out what happened to your parents. You could be in a lot of danger. Never open the door that way again until we have this cleared up."

"Oh, sorry. Come in. I've got a gun."

Rutger was five-ten, solidly built with dark hair, a moustache and long side burns and he wore eyeglasses.

"Pack up anything you unpacked," Spur said. "We're finding you a better room. One on the third floor in the corner at the end of a hall. Easier to defend."

"I don't think that will be necess—"

He stopped when Spur glared at him.

"It doesn't matter what you think right now, Rutger. I want you alive for a few more hours so we can talk. Let's start as you pack. Did your parents say anything to you about selling the ranch?"

"No."

"Did they say anything about moving anywhere for any reason?"

"Not once. I'm sure something terrible has happened to them. Mother would never—" He choked it off.

"Would they have told you if they were going to visit relatives, or if relatives were in trouble and needed their help?"

"Yes, we talked about everything. Finances, weather, the way the meat prices were, how we could run the ranch better. I went to school so I could do it better. Learning business and government and I even took some animal husbandry courses."

Spur picked up the bag that Rutger finished packing and opened the door. He looked both ways, waited a minute, then hurried the young man down the hallway and up the steps to the third floor. There was only one stairway, a central one. Spur checked the end room on floor three one way. It was locked and occupied.

The end room the other way down the hall was open and not used. He put Rutger in there, gave him the key and told him to lock the door. Then Spur went down to the room clerk. For five dollars the room clerk made a notation that room 313 was out of service, needing repairs.

Back upstairs Spur knocked on the door.

"Who is it?" Rutger asked.

Spur responded and the youth opened the door. Spur showed him how to put the straight backed chair under the door knob as an added protective measure.

They talked for a half hour. Slowly Spur impressed on the young man the danger he was in. He was never to go to the dining room, but have his meals brought up to his room. He was not to go on the street or to wear a gun.

"No gun? I don't understand?"

"The Circle S riders are not the ones you know. All the old hands have vanished and new ones are out there. Yesterday they tried three times to kill me, and my last name isn't even Shuntington. Whoever rustled your whole ranch doesn't want you showing up to cause trouble. Their best plan will be to kill you as soon as they know you're in town."

"I understand. I'm certain that dad would never sell the ranch, at least not without calling me home and explaining to me why and what else we were planning. He told me time and time again that the ranch would be mine to run when I grow up. He said when I came home from college we'd run it together, make it the biggest and best cattle ranch in all of Wyoming and then of the whole West!"

"I hope you still get the chance. Now, I understand you have a sister away at school. Would she come dashing back here if she heard about this?"

"Yes, I'm sure she would. Priscilla is a level headed young woman. She's just a year younger than I am. She wanted to go to college, too. She's in Denver."

"Who was your father's closest friend in town?"

"Easy, the banker, Ira Villary. A good man. Always fair in his dealings with us."

"Anybody else?"

"We had a lawyer, Elliot Parker. Dad used him because he said he was the only one of the three lawyers in town who knew anything about the law. Requirements aren't very strict yet in the territory for lawyers to practice. Dad sort of wanted me to go read for the law, but I wanted a better, broader education."

"What about the doctor?"

"That would be old Doctor Asamore. He's the only one in town and I guess he's all right. Delivers babies and sets broken arms, but he isn't much for cutting people open.''

"How is he on bullet wounds?"

"Dad said he was good at that. He gets enough practice.''

"What I was waiting to hear. I've got a shot up leg I need to have checked. First thing we're going to do is see the banker, then the lawyer, and if we have time, the doctor.

"Get a hat to cover up your face, then we'll stick to the alleys and try to stay alive. Ready?''

For a moment a flicker of fear crossed the young man's face. Then he scowled and nodded. Rutger Shuntington was going to do all right, Spur decided.

5

As soon as Rutger Shuntington entered the bank by
the side door right behind Spur McCoy, the bank
owner saw him and motioned to the back. They went
through a door into a private room near the vault
and the rather tall banker with black hair pasted
across a bald spot and horn rimmed glasses shook
his head.

"Rutger Shuntington, as I live and breathe. Never
thought I'd see hide nor hair of you again. I do hope
you have some word about your parents. We're all
extremely worried about them around Laramie."

Rutger frowned and then lifted his brows. "Mr.
Villary, I'm afraid I came here hoping you could
give me some idea of what happened to my parents.
I know nothing."

"Oh, dear!" Ira Villary's eyes bulged in despair,
then he motioned to a seat beside a big desk and
dropped into the fancy, padded chair behind it. "I
was hoping. . . ." He looked away. "Well, I guess
we'll just have to. . . ." Villary shook his head again
and stared out a small window fronted on a brick
wall next door. The bank building evidently had
been put up first when the window had a worthwhile
view.

"Do the Shuntingtons still have an account at

your bank, Mr. Villary," Spur asked.

The man looked up coldly.

"I'm afraid I don't know who you are. I've heard that a stranger came to town asking a lot of questions and getting shot at. Are you that individual?"

"Yes, Spur McCoy is my name. Is there still a Shuntington account here?"

"No, I'm afraid not. As soon as I heard that Rutger came to town I checked that file time and time again." He tapped a manila folder on his desk.

"The record shows that a check was drawn against the Circle S Ranch account, signed by Oliver Shuntington for the sum of six-hundred and forty-seven dollars. Two days later a man who identified himself with letters as one Archibald Pumetter, cashed the instrument here at the bank. The signature of Oliver Shuntington matched my records, the gentleman's papers were in order, so of necessity and a matter of law, I paid out the check."

"How much was in the account at that time?" Rutger asked.

"Six-hundred and fifty-seven dollars," the banker answered. "That left ten dollars as the balance."

Rutger walked to the door and came back. His face was sullen and angry, but when he looked up, his features softened.

"Mr. Villary, I'm not blaming you. But I'd say we have been swindled by someone, the family bank account emptied, and the family ranch rustled—not just the cattle, the whole thing!"

"At the time there wasn't a hint of anything devious or illegal," the banker said.

"I'm sure there wasn't, Mr. Villary," Rutger said. "I'm not blaming you. They planned it that way. All I can hope is that this is their last crime and that they soon step onto a gallows and feel the bite of a rope."

"Mr. Villary, I'm with the United States Secret Service sent here by Washington D.C. to investigate this matter. Could I look at the check and the signature card, please?"

"The Secret Service? I thought you were supposed to prevent counterfeiting." He blinked. "Yes, yes, right away."

A few minutes later Spur and Rutger left the bank and walked slowly down the street.

"It doesn't look good, does it, Mr. McCoy?"

"No. The more I see, the more worried I become that your parents are in terrible danger."

"Not danger, Mr. McCoy. I'm afraid they both must be dead. My father would never stand for this sort of a sale of what he has called the family's home place. He planned on this ranch staying in the Shuntington family for five-hundred years. The check proves it to me. My father would never let anyone else write a check on his bank account. Not even mother. And that was not his writing on the check. I'm positive of that. He might have to write twenty drafts, but he always did it himself. He learned to read and write late in life and he was proud of his accomplishment. It meant a lot to him."

"Who is the lawyer you mentioned?"

"Elliot Parker. Dad knew him for four or five years, I guess. He came out to the ranch every so often. Dad signed papers and they talked about new land and buying more land along the river.

"Whoever controls the Laramie river around here, controls all the grazing land in this section of Wyoming. Dad wanted to own land on both sides of the Laramie river, right up to the North Platte."

"That's a big spread."

"Yeah, big enough for somebody to spend a lot of time figuring out how to steal it. Somebody rustled not only our cattle but our land deed and the whole damn Circle S ranch!"

"If that's true, Rutger, we need to find out how they did it, who they are, and come up with the best way to win back your rights to the Circle S."

"Can't be an easy job. They've been here two months now. That's an old trail to follow."

"I've followed lots harder trails. Where is the lawyer?"

The law office perched on the second floor over the dress shop. A wag once told Spur that lawyers roosted on one floor off the street so no drunks would stagger in the door and ask to be represented. If a client could climb the steps, he should be sober enough to have saved some cash money for legal fees.

Spur turned the doorknob and the two men walked inside. It was a man's room. The office was only ten-feet square, but it was entirely paneled with some dark varnished wood. Around three sides were hunting trophy heads.

Spur recognized the shaggy head of a buffalo, a moose with its thick webbed antlers, and a prong horn antelope. On the far wall all to itself the white head of a mountain sheep stared down at Spur.

Across the room a man sat behind a solid oak desk. He looked up and rose at once. His vest was open showing a white shirt. A black suit coat hung on a hook behind him. Deep, dark eyes flared in a sudden reaction and his face showed worry.

"Rutger Shuntington! I'm surprised to see you here."

He came forward and gripped Rutger's hand. "I hope you can explain to me about your parents and the Circle S."

Rutger shook his head. "I thought you would be the only one in town who knew what happened. I understand someone says he bought the ranch. Is that right?"

"I'm as much in the dark as everyone else. I even had an appointment with your father on a Friday. I started to ride out to the ranch and someone stopped me at gunpoint, turned me around and said the ranch was now owned by someone else."

"Oh, Elliot Parker, this is Spur McCoy, a friend of mine. I don't think you've met."

The men shook hands briefly, Parker's glance resting too long on Spur. He looked back at Rutger.

"Is it true then, that you have no idea why your parents sold the Circle S, and especially why they pulled up and left the state in the dead of night?"

"Yes, Mr. Parker. I don't know now, but you can bet that I'm going to find out before too damn long. That ranch was the only reason I went away to college. I was coming back and planning on making the Circle S into the biggest spread in the whole state of Wyoming!"

Spur moved into the conversation quickly.

"Mr. Parker, didn't Mr. Shuntington say anything at all about moving? Maybe about some family problems back east. I understand you were the family lawyer. Did he make out a will or change any legal papers? How about his coming to you to raise some money by selling some land?"

"Yes, there was that about some money a week or so before. But I never thought much about it. Oliver was always getting together three or four thousand dollars to buy up a homestead of some little rancher or some creek bottom farmer who gave up and wanted to get back to Chicago or even Nebraska."

"How much was he trying to raise last you knew?" Rutger asked.

"I think it was eight-thousand dollars. He figured he'd sell off eight-hundred head of steers and have plenty."

"Ten dollars a head?" Spur asked.

"Been the going price lately. Railroad's made a

glut of beef on the Chicago market so the price came down."

Rutger stood and walked around the room. "You're still my lawyer, Mr. Parker. I'll pay you somehow. I want you to try to find any chinks in the papers that were filed on the ranch. Any way at all that I could sue this new owner. After that we'll think of some other way to get at him."

"Well, you sound determined, young Shuntington."

"It's my ranch. If Dad is gone, then it's my responsibility. I know dad would never walk away from his dream, not a chance in hell! Somebody might have driven him off, shot at him, something. You can be damn certain that I'm going to find out, and take care of the situation."

He walked around the room again. "Your first job is to check those legal papers, and the deed. See if it's really my father's signature or if it's a forgery. I'll be in touch."

Rutger walked out of the room and Spur followed. Spur caught up with him on the steps.

"You laid it on pretty hard in there, Rutger."

"True, I wanted to see his reaction. Also, I want to see what he will do. I've never liked the man. I caught him fondling my sister when she was sixteen. I wouldn't trust him to file his own death certificate."

They went across the street and into the Johnson Dry Goods store.

"I want to watch out the window and see if Parker leaves his place."

"Is there a back stairs?" Spur asked.

"Oh, yeah."

"I'll cover it." Spur walked out the front door, hurried across the street to a saloon and went through it and into the alley. He stepped behind a pile of pasteboard boxes just as Elliot Parker strode out the back door of his office, down wooden steps and marched down the alley away from Spur.

The lawyer went into the back door next to the brick building down the way. Spur checked it. Second establishment from the corner. He walked around to main street and saw that the second business was the Tumbleweed Saloon. Interesting. The lawyer suddenly had a big thirst. Or did he?

Spur leaned against the store across the street with a sign that identified it as: "I. J. Locklear, Dentistry." He pulled his hat down to shade his eyes and hide most of his face.

Five minutes later a man came out of the Tumbleweed Saloon, jumped on a horse and moved out of town to the north. Spur saw the fresh Circle S brand on the nag's hip. He wished he knew exactly why this Circle S rider came out of the saloon so quickly after Elliot Parker went in the back door.

Elliot Parker swore as soon as the door closed to his office on the second floor and Rutger Shuntington walked out. The kid was giving the orders now? Christ, there was gonna be shit flying over this! The kid wasn't even supposed to come back home until school was over at the end of the summer. Curt was going to shit green and puke purple.

Parker locked the front door, grabbed his hat and jammed it on as he went out the back door making sure it locked. He charged down the steps to the alley and up six doors to the Tumbleweed Saloon.

Once inside he turned left and took the steps three at a time. His key opened a lock and he slumped down behind an old desk in a chair with a feather pillow.

"Zeke!" he bellowed.

A razor blade thin man walked in with a small bar towel over his arm.

"Yeah, boss?"

"A cold beer and get Terry up here pronto."

Zeke had seen Parker in this mood before. He vanished, grabbed a bottle of cold beer from the ice box and waved at Terry who stood at the bar.

"Boss wants you upstairs, right now."

"He look mad?"

"Damn mad, if'n you ask me. Take the cold beer up to him, that might cool him down a mite."

Terry grabbed the bottle of beer and hurried up the steps. He pushed into the small office and looked at Parker, then took a step backward.

"Give me the damn beer!" Parker bellowed. He had written a note and now folded it and put it in an envelope. In it he had told Curt Cameron exactly what was going on in town, including the sudden appearance of the son of the former Circle S owner. They both knew the trouble that made.

They both knew the trouble that made.

"Now we are in a hell of a mess. Get those cattle rounded up at once so we can sell them and get moving!"

Parker didn't sign the note. Just pushed it in the envelope, sealed it and folded the white protector once. He looked up at Zeke and scowled.

"You get this into Curt's hand, and no other, or I'll cut your whang off, you understand me, Zeke?"

"Yeah, right. Got it. You want me to ride straight out there or meander around a little?"

"Straight as a rifle bullet, and just as fast. Move!" The sudden shouted word rolled Zeke out of the office and sent him running down the steps. He didn't even take time to grab a cold bottle of beer before he hurried out to the street and climbed on board his old dun gelding and spurred him out of town to the north.

Parker watched him go, then went down the stairs and checked the poker tables. The man he wanted wasn't there. It took Parker a half hour to find Weldon. Only name he'd ever known the man by. Parker pulled out a chair at a penny ante game in a saloon down the street and tossed a dime in the pot. The dealer dealt him a hand of five card stud.

"Weldon, the Circle S has five-thousand head of prime beef. You buying?"

"Sometimes. Not when I'm card playing."

"It's penny ante, for Christ sakes."

"Poker is poker. After the game."

When the hand was over, Weldon nodded. "Got a wire this morning. Chicago is stuffed with beef. You got any sheep or hogs?"

"Hell, no."

"Can't buy any steers for three days. No cattle cars to get out this far. Used them up in Dodge and the rest of Kansas. You get me a hundred box cars and I'll buy every steer you can beg, borrow or rustle."

"Three days?"

"At least three days."

"Can you ship five-thousand?"

"Can you round up five-thousand?"

"Yes."

"Get them here, I'll buy them. Now, let's play some real poker. Nickel a bump."

Elliot Parker stood up and snorted in disgust. He didn't want to play poker. He had much bigger game to stalk. He went out the back door and down to his law office.

Spur had watched Elliot Parker go from saloon to saloon. At last the lawyer failed to leave one drinking emporium, and Spur found Rutger still in Johnson Dry Goods pacing up and down and showing his anger and impatience.

"Dinner time back at the hotel," Spur said. "I'll bring it up to your room."

Spur had just brought the plates back down to the dining room when he saw an old friend.

"Frank Weldon, you old shyster gone bad. Is this your territory now?"

The cattle buyer stared at Spur for a moment, then stuck out his big hand. "McCoy, be damned. Ain't seen you since Dodge. You still working the lawman angle?"

"Seem to be. You been here long?"

"Two years."

"Then you knew the Shuntingtons."

"Much as anybody. Kept to themselves a bit."

"What happened to them?"

"Damned if I know. One day they were here, next day gone and a new man running things. His name is Curt Cameron. Fact is, I just made a deal for five-thousand head of his steers soon as he can get them to the stock yard."

Rutger Shuntington had come up behind where the men were speaking.

"No! It can't be! If he sells off five-thousand head, that will bring our level of good breeding stock too low. He's got to be cutting into the breeding stock to sell that many this time of the year!"

Frank Weldon looked up surprised.

"Rutger Shuntington, Frank. He's the man who should know about his father's herd."

Rutger set his jaw. "I was hoping you could tell us what happened to my parents, Mr. Weldon. Dad and mom both gone, and this wild man selling off the herd! He's looting the ranch of everything we own. I won't stand for it!

"McCoy, we've got to figure out how to stop this bastard before he ruins the Circle S!"

6

Blade Gunnison sat naked on the edge of the bed and cleaned his fingernails with his eight-inch hunting knife. The blade glistened from honing and Gunnison claimed he could shave with it. He only proved it on a bet.

Blade belched and wiped a dribble of saliva from his mouth. The woman on the bed beside him yawned.

"When the hell you gonna get to it, Blade? I ain't got all day for a fucking two dollars."

"Shut up your face, Petite, or I'll slap it shut!" Gunnison took a swing at her but the woman fell back away from the blow.

"Come on, Blade, you ain't got your money's worth yet. You got it in you for a second time or you done blew your whole wad with one fuck?"

"Day I can't cum twice, bitch, is the day I try for three."

"Show me," La Petite growled at him. She spread her legs and lifted her knees and grinned. La Petite had named herself when she first came to The Sewing Circle whorehouse two years ago when they were still in a tent. She stood a little over five-feet eleven, was big boned and slightly chunky, weighing a sturdy one-hundred and seventy pounds. Her

breasts billowed out like ripe melons even when she
lay flat on her back.

"Show me, little man."

He slapped her breast, his face purple. "Don't you
ever call me that again!" he roared. At once he
dropped between her heavy thighs and jabbed at her
crotch. When he plunged in he snorted.

"Damn, La Petite, you're half cunt, you know
that? Half cunt and the rest tits and mouth."

"Whatever you say, Blade. Now show me what a
big man you really are."

Blade grunted, drew up his knees outside of her
thighs and pounded against her. By that time he
was so angry at her that it didn't take long.

Ten ramming hard strokes and he went off like a
premature dynamite charge.

La Petite brushed back dark hair from her face
and laughed. "Oh, hell yes, Blade, you're a big
fucking man. You must be at least seven-feet tall!"
Her laugh roared out again and Blade reached over
the side of the bed for his belt.

His hand came back with his eight-inch knife and
he laid the razorlike edge of it against her throat.

"You got to do one more thing for me, whore. I
always wanted to kill a fucking whore while I was
inside her. Know what I mean? I think now is the
right time. Whole territory of Wyoming be hell of a
lot better off without you around."

La Petite lay totally still. Only her eyes moved.
She watched his sadistic, leering face.

"Come on, Blade, just a little joke. A girl's got
feelings too, you know."

"You feel with your crotch and think with your
pussy." He stared at her a moment, then snorted.
"Hell no. I'm not wasting my great idea on some big
horse like you. I want me a small little pretty thing
with a lot to live for. Horses like you just fuck and

breed and get sent out to pasture or turned into soap."

He moved the knife down to her breasts and sliced a three-inch line a quarter-inch deep across one. Blood flowed at once and La Petite lunged away and screamed louder than any woman he had ever heard.

Blade jerked out of her, pulled on his pants and jammed on his boots. The whore on the bed continued to scream. Before he had on his shirt, Blade saw the door edge open.

Barney stood there staring. Barney was slow witted. He looked at the blood, then at Blade.

"Barney, kill the bastard!" La Petite screamed. "He cut me bad! Kill the fucking bastard! Take out that six-gun and give it to me if you won't use it!"

Blade moved toward Barney shaking his head.

"Don't do anything, Barney. Not your fight. Just turn around and go tell that old bitch downstairs it's no problem. Go on, get out of here!"

Barney loomed a foot over the five-foot four enforcer for the Circle S ranch. Barney shook his head.

"Blood," he said. "No hurt girls, no blood."

"Get out of here you halfwit. Move, damnit!"

Blade got his shirt on and slammed his fist into Barney's gut. The man was slow mentally, but not physically. He was as strong as a big draft horse. Blade's fist felt like he had hit an iron wall.

Slowly Barney stepped toward Blade. "You come," he said.

Blade snorted, swiped his knife toward the big man who didn't even try to dodge. The keen edge sliced a wound a half-inch deep across Barney's thick forearm.

Barney looked at the blood on his arm. He growled. His eyes went wide for a moment, then he walked toward Blade. The big knife rammed forward, Blade's wrist and arm forming a straight line with the weapon as it grated off a rib and plunged deep into Barney's chest.

Blade jerked it out and reversed the motion and before La Petite could scream again, the razor-edge sliced across Barney's throat, severing both carotid arteries. Blood spurted from the tubes, splashing across the room from the intense pressure in the slow witted man's blood lines. His eyes went wide again, he looked at Blade, then at La Petite. His hand started to come up, then ten seconds after his throat slash, Barney crumpled to the floor in a pile of lifeless bone and muscle.

La Petite forgot her wound. She darted around both men and ran down the hall, naked and screaming.

Blade looked at her a minute, then glanced out the window. If the sheriff came he'd have to explain. Instead of the sheriff, Blade saw Spur McCoy walk out of a store and turn into the seamstress lady's shop. Why in hell was he heading in there? Blade caught at his rifle that stood beside the door, but by the time he got it aimed, the doorway to the shop stood empty.

Blade snarled, cleaned the knife off on the dead man's shirt and ran for the stairs. He met the old whore herself, Wanda, as she charged up the steps from the first floor.

"What you been doing, Blade?" she shrilled.

Blade slapped her to one side and ran down the stairs, out the front door and headed for the seamstress shop. He hesitated before he went in. He'd never been in such an establishment before.

Then he thought of his quarry just inside and slammed the door open as he bolted in, his six-gun raised and cocked.

Blade stopped just past the door and looked

around. Bolts of cloth, strange looking half women forms with no heads standing on wire devices, some with part of a fancy dress on them. At the side he saw a head bob up from her lock stitch Singer sewing machine.

Fear flared across Amy York's face as she saw the gun.

She stood slowly, her face nearly white now. "Yes?" she asked in a soft voice.

Blade ignored her, stared around at the small shop, trying to find out where Spur hid. He found no possible location. A door at the back stood half open. Blade charged it, came into an empty room another forty-feet deep that had a door in the rear.

No spot showed where the man could be hiding, so Blade rushed to the door and stared out cautiously. No one showed in the alley. Blade swore, went back in the shop and stood in front of the seamstress.

"Where the hell is he?"

"I beg your pardon?"

"That man who just came in here. Where the fu— Where did he go?"

"Out the back, the same way you went. Why?"

"None of your business. It ain't healthy in this town to know that gent. See that you don't."

"I don't know who you are, sir," Amy said, her color coming back and rising to a red surge, "but I'll be friends with anyone I wish to. The likes of you will never tell me what to do."

"Damn uppity female! I've had enough of your kind today!" Blade whirled and stormed out the front door. The force of his exit jerked two screws out of wood that held the bottom of the screen door in place.

Amy sighed and looked after him as he marched down the boardwalk.

Blade fumed as he walked. What the hell? He

could have had a shot at the bastard if he hadn't been fucking around with that damn halfwit! Blade slid into a chair outside of the Tumbleweed Saloon, tipped back against the wall and watched the street. The fucker had to come out sometime and go into the hotel. That would be his last mistake!

Blade growled at anyone who approached him. Two riders from the Circle S tried to talk to him and he waved them away with insults. He had a job to do and so far he hadn't got it done. Who would have guessed the asshole would have stayed in somebody else's room the other night when the dynamite went off? Damn lucky for him.

Blade spent half the day watching the street, checking everyone on the boardwalk, and viewing the front and side doors of the Medicine Bow Hotel, but Spur McCoy had not shown up. Just like the bastard to get a room on the ground floor back so he could go in and out the window into the alley.

Blade belched. He was hungry. He sat there on the chair for a minute more, looked across at the small cafe on the other side of the street and at last gave in. As he walked across the dusty, horse-dropping littered avenue, he spotted four more Circle S riders spaced down the boardwalk. They were all hunting for Spur McCoy. The man who brought McCoy's head to Curt earned a fifty-dollar bounty.

Good hunting.

There were at least five more men in town. Not even Blade knew where they hid. In case of a shoot, there would be plenty of friendly guns from the company.

Blade ate a steak, three vegetables and four slices of thick cut bread. He sopped up the gravy with the last slab of bread and looked at the kitchen.

Enough. He had to be able to walk, even run if he found McCoy. He paid and left the eatery. Two more

of the Circle S riders drifted into the cafe. Nobody
spoke to anybody else.

Blade Gunnison belched again, grinned and
settled down on the bench outside the hardware
store. It was almost in the center of town and he
could see both ways a block and a half to the end of
the three-year-old village. Not one hell of a lot here
yet. Might be some day.

He pulled the big knife out and cleaned his fingernails again, then he stabbed the blade into the inch-
thick boards that formed the walkway. Hell, he
might have to wait until dark . . . again.

Spur McCoy had made three quick trips to the
town section that afternoon. Each was short, and he
kept to the alleys and stores as much as possible.
Twice he had left the jail by the back door. On the
last trip he went to the hotel and discovered that
Rutger Shuntington had left his room. So far Spur
hadn't found him. He just hoped that he ran down
the young man before some Circle S rider figured
out who he was.

At least all of the Circle S riders were strangers,
and didn't know Rutger. That could explain why the
young man was still alive. Spur came through the
alley and up to the street where the bank stood. He
peered around the corner and down the boardwalk.
It was still light, maybe six-thirty.

A look east proved unproductive. He glanced the
other way and spotted Rutger coming out of the gun
shop. The lean young man settled a new gunbelt on
his hips, adjusted the feel of the holster with its load
of a six-gun.

Spur walked out of the alley, strode down the
boardwalk close to the buildings and caught Rutger
around the shoulder and propelled him on down the
street. They walked straight for the hardware store.

Too late Spur saw Blade Gunnison let his chair drop to the boardwalk and come up with a fist full of iron as he stood.

Spur pushed Rutger out of the way and drew. His thumb cocked the hammer as he grabbed the weapon and in one smooth almost effortless move brought it upward, out of leather. The split second the muzzle cleared the holster he swung it up and his finger caressed the trigger.

Spur's .44 round caught Gunnison in the left shoulder and drove him back against the wall.

Two more men down the street ran forward, six-guns in their hands.

Blade twisted around, lifted his pistol again, but before he could fire, Spur grabbed Rutger and jerked him into Johnson's Dry Good store. They ran through the store and out the back into the alley.

Two men were already down the alley waiting for them. Both lifted guns and Spur and Rutger's irons snarled at about the same time. One of the men went down, the other dodged behind a pile of cordwood.

Spur dove in back of a corner of building and Rutger crouched behind a garbage barrel.

"I'm hit, Jessie Bob! Give me a hand." The voice came with a wail of pain.

The other man fired twice into the barrel, then darted for another cover. Spur fired once and the running Circle S rider went down as a .44 slug slammed through his spinal column.

For a moment it was quiet. Then from behind them a man snarled and Rutger sprinted for the safety of the building.

"The other direction," Rutger whispered. "Another one of them."

"Might be eight or ten Circle S riders in town," Spur said. "Part of the reason I wanted you inside and out of sight."

"Couldn't stand it any longer cooped up that way."

"Better than shot dead."

Spur leaned around the building and fired twice down the alley, then reloaded the empty rounds to put six in the chambers.

A rifle snarled a shot down the alley from the direction of the dead man. Spur pulled back farther. Rutger leaned out to fire down the alley at the six-gun man when a round jolted into his shoulder and tumbled him backward.

Spur grabbed him and pulled him to safety before the marksman could fire again. Spur checked the wound. The lead slug had only grazed Rutger's upper arm. Spur wrapped his kerchief around the wound tightly and tied the ends.

"That will hold it for a while."

"Hurt like hell. I don't want to get shot again."

Spur eyed their situation. No way out, gunmen on both ends. He saw at once that there was no back door in the building they were backed up against. Like rats in a trap.

Almost. Spur spotted the ladder at the end of the building. They could go up and over the roof without either man seeing them. Spur pointed at the ladder and asked Rutger if he could do it with one arm. The young man gritted his teeth from the pain in his arm.

"I can . . . got to or die." He ran for the ladder.

Spur sent a bullet each way every two or three minutes. Soon there were two guns on each end of the alley. He let more time go between rounds. Then when he was sure Rutger was up the ladder, he fired once more and ran for the boards nailed up the side of the building.

Spur climbed. He was almost at the top when someone shouted below and behind him. He whirled almost at the roof line. A six-gun fired once from below. Spur drew and kicked out two rounds at the Circle S man, knocked him down with the second, and rolled over the parapet to the roof.

Thirty-feet across the roof, Rutger stood at the open door that led downward. Spur joined him and they soon were in the second floor over the General store. The stairs were inside, and they stayed in the store for a half hour. Spur and Rutger both bought new shirts and hats and left their old ones in the store. A little change in appearance right now might work. They left separately, ambling up the street toward the first alley.

Spur had insisted that Rutger come to the jail to stay that night. He offered little objection.

"Hell, don't worry about your shoulder. We'll stop by at that doctor friend of yours, Asamore. I hope he's good."

They made it to the first alley, slipped in and watched. Two men ran down the street and talked with a short man who had a new bandanna bandage around his upper left arm. Three of them talked a bit, then scattered, after reloading their six-guns.

Rutger led Spur to the back door of the doctor's office. Just as they came out of the alley, a gunman laughed and stepped out from some shrubs, his gun coming up.

Spur shot him before he could fire. The round drilled through his chest and heart, missed his back bone and lodged in the side of the house next to him.

Spur pushed open the door and moved into the doctor's back room. Rutger's color was fading. His new shirt sleeve was soaked with blood even after the quick repair job in the General Store.

A man came in wearing a suit and a frown. He was medium sized, lots of gray hair, a paunch and a frown.

"Figured somebody broke in back here." He looked back at Rutger. "It is you, the Shuntington boy, Rutger, right? Hope to hell you can tell us what happened to your parents."

"First let's see what you can do for his fresh gunshot wound. It's not serious. Then if you've got time, I want you to check over some amateur nurse's work on another bullet hole, mine."

Doc Asamore took off Rutger's shirt and frowned.

"Wish you'd quit playing with guns. Never helped a soul a bit. Give me too much work to do." He doused the wound with alcohol and Rutger whimpered, then passed out where he sat in a chair.

Doc grunted and then probed the graze wound in Rutger's upper arm.

"Guess the lead is all out. Sliced up some skin. About all." He worked on the wound, and watched Spur.

"You're the stranger in town who's trying to find out what happened to Ollie Shuntington, I reckon. They didn't leave town of their own accord, I can vouch for that. Guess I can tell now. Mrs. Shuntington had a tumor, bad one. Couldn't do nothing but make her more comfortable. She was on laudanum."

He looked up. "You know that's just watered down opium. I don't like to use it because a patient can get to depend on it. Terrible stuff, but it does make a body forget about the pain, and Mrs. Shuntington was in constant pain. Only way we could relieve it. Nobody in town knew. She was getting a new dress made for a party they had planned. I think she figured it might be her last party."

"Did either of them say anything about moving, selling out, going away?" Spur asked.

"Not a single word. I'm certain Ollie wouldn't

have made his wife suffer that way. Nope, they're
either prisoners out there or they're both dead.
Goldarnit, you can bank on that."

A few minutes later Doc had Rutger's wound
bandaged and the young man had regained consciousness. Dr. Asamore looked at Spur's thigh
wound, scraped off a little dead skin and put on
some salve and rebandaged it.

"Whoever did that the first time knew what he
was doing," Doc said. "You was lucky it was a clean
through shot." When he finished he took the pair of
greenback dollar bills Spur gave him.

"I could get spoiled, getting paid for my services.
Come back every time you get shot," he snorted.
"Actually, I'd rather not see you again in that the
case." Doc Asamore sobered. "McCoy, do what you
can to find out about Ollie and his missus. They was
good folks. I'm just feared we won't see them
again."

Rutger was a little woozy but he stood and he
could walk. They went round about and it was just
getting dark when they walked into the back door of
the jail.

"Sheriff, have a new customer for you. He was
firing his pistol in the city limits."

Sheriff Dryer grunted. He pushed a paper over to
Spur. "Sign it, you got to be in on this last shooting,
right? In the alley in back of the General Store. Kid
was from the Circle S. Never did get his name. The
other Circle S riders tied him over a horse and lit
out. Figured it had to be you."

"One more gun we won't have to face when we
charge the Circle S," Spur said.

Sheriff Dryer looked up quickly as if trying to
figure out if Spur were serious or not.

Spur never told him.

7

Priscilla Shuntington sniffed daintily and moved away from the man who sat beside her on the Union Pacific railroad passenger coach. Her journey was almost over and she was looking forward to seeing her brother.

The letter that had finally arrived with the telegram in it from Sheriff Dryer was most unsettling. She had heard from her parents a month before. They were fine, the Spring roundup was getting started and everything was progressing nicely.

Then the letter came from the sheriff. She had taken a stage coach from Denver up to Cheyenne, then boarded the train. This trip numbered only her second ride and she enjoyed the fifty-mile run to Laramie. Even if one man had been more than friendly. At last she had taken a pair of scissors from her purse and laid them in her lap as she pretended to sew a button on.

Every time the man tried to talk to her, she picked up the scissors holding them like a knife. The man had soon moved to another seat. This current swain seemed not so easily discouraged.

"Now, miss. You don't have to hold those scissors like you're about to run me through. We both know you won't do that, because I'm just a friendly gent who likes to talk to beautiful girls. And you're about the prettiest thing I've seen in a month of Saturdays."

She turned and looked out the window trying to hide a small smile of pleasure at his compliment. "Sir, I am not speaking with you. I made that clear."

He grinned. He appeared to be about twenty-five, wore a suit, white shirt and tie and carried a case. Some kind of a drummer. He even sounded like a salesman.

"All that wonderful blonde hair and the way it's curled so nice is certainly your crowning glory, Miss. Are you traveling far? I noticed that you got on at Cheyenne."

She stared out the window, but the faint smile was still there.

"Fact is, what a beautiful lady like you needs is somebody to protect her on a trip like this. I'll be glad to volunteer for the position without any compensation whatsoever."

She turned and pointed the scissors at him. "Then you won't mind being my bodyguard from across the aisle. I need that space to lay out my sewing."

"Sewing? All I see is a bunch of buttons."

"Please let me lay out my things." Priscilla hesitated. "We can even talk."

"Great!" He moved across the aisle, she covered the seat beside her with some sewing and talked with him the last ten miles. He was a salesman heading for Laramie and points west.

When Priscilla detrained at Laramie, she lost the young man who had to find his sample cases. Priscilla had brought with her only a small carpet bag. She could get her other clothes at the ranch.

Priscilla pulled her bag from under the seat and hurried off the train and over to the Medicine Bow

Hotel. She would stay there until she talked with the sheriff and the lawyer. The family counselor must know something about all this.

She told the room clerk to register her on the second floor, left her bag with him and marched straight over to the lawyer's office. She remembered it was on the second level. Parker, that was his name.

Elliot Parker looked up warily when Priscilla came in the door of his office. When he saw her, he jumped to his feet at once. There weren't any girls as pretty as this one in half the state. He recognized Priscilla Shuntington at once. He'd been smitten with her for the past four years.

"Miss Shuntington! Priscilla! How nice to see you!"

She colored slightly. Priscilla remembered the day at the ranch by the well house when he had kissed her lips and then fondled her breasts. Priscilla had been young and curious. The incident still embarrassed her.

"Yes, Mr. Parker, it's good to see you too. Now what is this all about that my parents have sold the ranch and moved?"

"I thought you knew all about it. Your father never consulted me. One day a new owner came in and said he wanted me to make sure the deed was signed correctly and to get it filed with the county clerk along with the bill of sale."

"What did Daddy tell you?"

"Nothing. I hadn't seen him for a week or two before that, and then the new owners came and your parents were gone. Somebody told me they went back to Kentucky to be with relatives."

"Our people live in Ohio."

"Maybe it was Ohio. It was such a surprise to everyone. I figured you and your brother would be the first ones to know about it."

"I don't. I want to hire you to find out exactly what is going on. I have money in a bank in Denver."

"Well, I don't know. Are you of legal age?"

"I'm twenty years old. I don't have to be twenty-one to hire you."

"Let's talk about it. First, are you set up in the hotel?"

"I left my bag there."

"Good. You'll have to stay there until this is settled. These new owners are at the Circle S ranch house. Let me take you over and get you settled in the hotel."

"I can handle that."

"No, no, I insist. It's the least I can do. Room clerks can be a bit difficult at times."

"Not Charley. I've known him for ten years."

Parker would not be dissuaded. He shut up his office, held her arm and guided her across the street past the strings and clumps of horse droppings, and to the boardwalk on the far side. She lifted her skirt to step up to the walk and she saw Parker watching for a flash of ankle.

At the hotel he made sure the room was right with the clerk, then took her bag and walked her down to it. It was on the second floor in back. Parker opened the door and let her go in.

"This will be quiet for you and not a lot of people dashing by your door." At once he closed the door and locked it.

Priscilla looked up at him in surprise. She was more shocked than anything. "Mr. Parker! This is not proper, you being in my hotel room this way with the door closed."

Before she could say another word, Parker pulled her into his arms and kissed her lips. His mouth devoured her, pressed her to him tightly so she could hardly breathe.

When she pulled her lips from his, she screamed. His hand came over her mouth quickly.

"No!" he said roughly. "No more damn screaming or teasing me. You're nothing but a cock tease and today you get what you deserve!"

He picked her up and threw her on the bed. Before she could recover from her surprise he had fallen on top of her, crushing her into the mattress, his hands ripping at the bodice of her dress until it tore apart and he pushed up her chemise revealing her breasts.

"Yes, great tits, I knew it. It's been four years since I've had my hands on them!"

Priscilla screamed again but his hand cut her off. He pulled a large handkerchief from his pocket and tied it around her head and across her open mouth.

"Now, no more screaming. Remember how it felt when I played with your tits in the well house? It's going to feel ten times as good now. Just relax, let it go. Enjoy it, because there is no way in hell that you can stop me."

He pulled off her dress, ripping it nearly in half to get it off her hips. Then he unbuttoned her regular drawers and pulled them down over her feet. He had pressed her hands under her back so she couldn't claw at him. She pulled one loose and scratched his cheek.

Parker slapped her hard, making her head swim for a moment. Then she realized he was right. She couldn't stop him, and he could beat her if she resisted. So she would go limp, not help him, not let him know she felt a thing. She would be like a wet dishcloth.

He spread her legs and at once realized she wasn't fighting him any more.

"Well, so you've come to your senses. Good. This

is what a woman is made for. And such a pretty one as you will enjoy it more and more." He took the gag from her mouth and she swallowed twice to get some moisture back in her mouth.

"Fucking is fun, Priscilla, remember that. Such great tits! Sit up and let me play with them."

He pulled her to a sitting position and marveled at the orbs that were full, with bright pink areolas and nipples. He sucked on them until he groaned with his own passion.

His lips strayed lower, then he pushed her flat and spread her legs.

"Beautiful!" His head dropped into her crotch and he kissed her sweet lips and groaned.

Then he pulled open his pants.

Priscilla couldn't look. Then she did and saw his long "thing" and her eyes widened in amazement. She'd never seen one before, not an erect, hard penis like his! So big. That huge, long thing couldn't possibly enter her!

She knew for sure. She had trouble sometimes getting just one of her fingers up her tight little pussy.

Before she knew it he was over her and his big cock pressing at her opening. She knew it wouldn't go in!

Then he spit in his hand and rubbed it on his long stick. How disgusting! It was the grossest thing she had ever seen!

But this time when he probed there was an opening. She felt a sharp pain and screeched. Then the pain was gone and a soft warm glow replaced it. She felt him sliding into her. It had happened! A man was making love to her! She had dreamed about being with a man, but never thought it would be like this!

She hated him.

She had to hate him because he was raping her. Yes, she hated him.

The soft, warm glow built and built. Her breasts warmed and then felt so hot she knew they were burning. He touched her nipples and they exploded. Her whole body shook and rattled and she humped her hips upward as fast as she could as the spasms drilled through her again and again.

The feeling intensified, becoming the most wonderful, the most thrilling and tremendous experience of her whole life! She wanted it to go on and on.

Three more times the spasms tore through her, setting her on fire, exploding all the old wives tales she had ever heard about sex. It was wonderful!

Still she hated him. It hadn't been her choice. He was good looking enough, it wasn't that. He wasn't her husband. Sex was for married people.

What if she got pregnant?

She refused to think about it. She noticed that Parker was pounding harder now, sweat dripped off his nose and hit her breasts. He humped her faster and faster until he groaned and snorted and brayed in delight as he thrust harder and she felt something hot jetting into her depths.

Suddenly he was done and pulled out of her. He sat on the bed beside her.

"Priscilla, I bet that was your first time, right?" She stared at the ceiling. She had to hate him.

"Don't worry, the next one will be better. We can make love a couple times a day if you want to. I know you'll be going back to school, but when this is all over about your parents, we can slip away and live together."

She sat up and slapped him hard on the face. He swayed to one side and when he came back, she slapped him again.

"Get out of my room, you bastard! As soon as I dress I'm going to the sheriff and charge you with rape."

He looked at her for a minute. "No, I don't think you will. It would ruin you in town. None of the women would ever speak to you again. The men would all try to seduce you knowing you had been had and were now public property, a kind of community chest. No, you won't even tell the sheriff about this, much less charge me with anything."

He stood and pulled his clothes around straight and buttoned up his fly.

"Besides, you'd never be able to prove it. I can find a dozen men who will swear I played cards with them all afternoon. I saw you to the desk clerk, made sure you had a good room, but I never went up the steps with you. Even the room clerk will swear to that for twenty-five dollars."

She slapped him again but he caught her hand before it hit. He pushed her back down on the bed and kissed her. She didn't help or stop him. He fondled her breasts again, then went to the door.

She lay there naked and spent on the bed and looked at him.

"Oh, yes, but you are a good fuck. Now you know it, too. I knew you would be great when I first played with your titties three, four years ago."

"Get out!" Priscilla shouted. "You try to touch me again and I'll kill you!"

"Not true, sweet pussy. Not true because I might be able to help you find your parents, and that's important to you. Just be careful who you tell about this little fuck. Certainly not your brother who might have some sense of chivalry and try to hurt me. Then I'd have to kill him."

He grinned and went to the door. "Take care of that great little body, especially that sweet, juicy

pussy!" He slipped out the door and Priscilla lay
there naked, spent, sexually satisfied as she had
never been before in her life.

She didn't know whether to laugh or to cry.
Instead she hugged herself, then sat up and looked
in her bag for a dress. She had just one other one.
The ripped one might be saved if it had torn apart at
the seams. She could take it to Amy, the seamstress.

Yes, that would work.

Priscilla sat there a moment thinking about her
experience. The first time! She hadn't wanted it to
be that way, but it had been thrilling, frightening,
shocking, yet tremendously satisfying as well. Had
she really been raped, or just roughly seduced? She
hadn't fought him very hard.

At last she slipped into her dress and decided not
to worry about it. Now she was more interested in
the next time, by a man who would be gentle and
giving and who would talk to her and explain things
as he went along. Yes, the Next Time!

It was still morning. The A.M. train had been
right on time, hitting the station at 9:05. Now it was
slightly after ten. She would go see the sheriff and
ask about her parents. Then she had no idea what
she would do.

Would she hire an investigator? Her father had
put three-thousand dollars in a Denver bank for her
when she decided to go to college there. Most of it
was left. She could write a draft on the Denver
account and cash it at Mr. Villary's bank here in
town. But who would she hire?

After dressing she looked at her hair. It hadn't
been mussed up much. Priscilla combed it thought-
fully, patted it in place. It swirled around her
shoulders now in a luxurious blonde sheath,
bounced on her forehead with bangs and flounced

down each side of her head with masses of curls.

Ready.

Strange, she had just been seduced/raped in one of the most terrifying/satisfying experiences of her life. Now she calmly combed her hair, adjusted her dress and got ready to go see the sheriff about her parents. Damn! She was growing up a little!

Sheriff Dryer shook his head at the pretty girl across his desk. "I'm sorry Miss Shuntington, I haven't been able to find a shred of evidence that your parents are still in the county. I wish I could. Your brother is in town, did you know that? He stayed in a cell here last night because the Circle S men are trying to shoot him."

"I guessed Rutger would come. Tell him I'm in the hotel." She stared at the law man. "Isn't there something we can do? Anything legally?"

"Not that I know of, Miss Shuntington. So far I have no evidence that a crime has been committed. the man has a legal bill of sale, the grant deed on the land has been signed over and registered with the county clerk. The ranch is his. Not a single reason for me to barge in there and demand to know what happened."

"But you knew my parents. They were your friends. How can you just let them vanish without a trace that way? Don't you wonder why they never came into town? Isn't it possible that the man who claimed he bought the ranch is really a killer who stole it and murdered my parents? Isn't that possible?"

Stan Dryer stood and walked around the room. He hated this part of his job. He stopped and watched the girl. She was strong, determined. She could get herself killed.

"Yes, Miss Shuntington, that is entirely possible. The chances are it's more than possible. The way the

Circle S men are rampaging around town, I'd say what you described is probably what has happened. The only problem is, there has to be some PROOF that it happened. Law depends on proving things. Right now I can't prove a single thing illegal took place.''

He waggled a finger at her. "And I don't want you to start messing in the picture. A government man is in town trying to figure it out. He got himself shot at three times the first day he was here.

"There has been at least one try to gun down your brother. These men are not playing games. So far half a dozen men have been killed. Most of them from the other side. I want you to be damned sure that you understand that this is a deadly affair."

"Yes, I understand that. I'd like to talk to this government man. Where is he staying?"

"The only safe place in town right now for him. Here at the jail."

'You mean it?''

"Of course. They dynamited his hotel room the first night. He got away."

Spur McCoy stepped into the sheriff's office, then saw Priscilla.

"Oh, sorry, Sheriff. Didn't know you had a visitor."

"Come in, McCoy. This is a lady you need to meet. Her name is Priscilla Shuntington."

Spur held his hat in one hand as he came in. He nodded to the woman. "I've been expecting you, Miss Shuntington. We're trying to sort out exactly what happened here."

"Do you think my parents are dead?"

Spur smiled, turned his hat. "You seem to be a very straight forward person, Miss Shuntington. There is a good chance that this is an outlaw band of some kind who conspired to take over the ranch.

Your parents may have been eliminated in the
process. These cowboys on your ranch seem more
like outlaws than range hands. They all shoot
exceptionally well, and are not afraid of a fight.
We're still trying to piece together what happened."

"Mr. McCoy, I want to know everything you do
about the problem. Can we have something to eat at
the hotel dining room and talk?"

"That's a little public for me, Miss Shuntington.
But there is a small restaurant down the street
where I've been eating in a back room. If that's all
right with you."

"Of course. Right now my job is to find out about
my parents. Sheriff, if my brother comes in, send
him to the same resturant, would you please?"

Sheriff Dryer nodded.

They ate and talked. Soon Spur had her up to date
on developments including his suspicions about the
lawyer. Priscilla seemed uncomfortable as he
described their talk with Parker.

"Yes, I know Mr. Parker. I never have trusted
him and never will. Would the outlaws have needed
a person here in town to do all of the paperwork for
them? If so, I wouldn't put it past Parker."

"Possible. He's on my list to watch. Right after
we talked to him yesterday a rider rushed out for the
ranch."

Spur stared at her. "How are we going to keep you
safe? There is no chance you can stay in the jail."

"Won't I be safe in the hotel?"

"Not if they decide that you'll be in the way, or a
threat to them." Spur shrugged. "Looks like you'll
have to move out of your room without telling the
clerk, and move into the room Rutger rented on the
third floor. No, we'll put you next door someplace
and I'll get the room beside you."

"You could stay in my room," she said quickly.
Then put her hand over her mouth. "I mean, I could
sleep in a chair and you could. . . ." She stopped and
laughed. "Oh dear. I shouldn't have said that. I
don't want you to think. . . ."

Spur laughed and shook his head. "I'm not
thinking anything about what you said. But, it
might be better if I had the adjoining room on the
third floor."

When the meal was over he sent her into the hotel
by the side door, and five minutes later he slipped in
the same way and went to the third floor. She was in
Rutger's room. He moved her bag to the room next
door, and then he occupied the one next to hers.

Spur pushed the heavy dresser in front of the
window. The tall model covered most of the glass
and would prevent anyone from breaking in that
way. He showed her how to set the chair under the
locked door.

"What you're telling me is you're not going to be
here for a while?"

"That's right. When it gets dark, I want to be
halfway out to the Circle S ranch. A little scouting
trip to see what I can find out."

"Be careful. May I call you Spur?"

"Yes, of course."

"You call me Priscilla." She hesitated. "Do you
need to run the risk of going out there?"

"Yes. I'll be back. Nobody has killed me yet."

Priscilla smiled boldly. "Spur, I'll be just terribly
mad if somebody does now. I want to get to know
you better."

"That sounds interesting. When I get back."

He went out the door, waited until he heard her
slide the chair under the knob, then slipped down
the stairs and headed for the livery stable by the

back way. If he left now, he would be only a few miles from the ranch when the sun went down. Night time, his time to prowl!

8

Spur McCoy eased out the side door of the hotel. He had scanned the side street both ways and left only when he was certain that there were no prowling gunmen or idlers who could be Circle S hands. He hurried down to the alley and headed for the back door of the hardware store.

Ten minutes later he left the establishment with six-feet of dynamite fuse, a dozen detonator caps and twenty sticks of dynamite. Stumps that needed blowing out, he had told the clerk.

Spur used his roundabout route to get to the livery stables at the edge of town, and saddled up his roan. He paid the livery man for the board and room and rode out to the south so he wouldn't go through town. He had a two hour wait before dark. This far north the sun stayed up a lot longer than it did in New Mexico.

Spur knew the stable hand was watching him. He skirted some brush near a small stream and when he rode out of sight, turned west toward the strip of green trees. He crossed the Union Pacific tracks and angled northwest toward the Laramie river.

It was a strange waterway. Headwaters were far to the south in Colorado. It ran north into Wyoming, then north through Laramie and angled

91

northeast at last into the North Platte River.

McCoy found a section he could ford and walked his roan through knee deep water to the far side.

Once behind the brush and cottonwoods along the stream, he felt more at ease. Spur took his time moving north. All of Laramie was now nearly a half mile on the far side of the river where it had built up around the railroad tracks.

He idled along, enjoying the coolness of the rushing water, a green ribbon in a semi-desert of high Wyoming plateau and the rolling start of the great range of mountains to the west.

Time would be slow to change this land. There was no reason to draw great numbers of people here. But Laramie would continue because it was a railroad town. The Southern Pacific had created Laramie to meet its fifty mile mandate from the government, and had left shops and workers here to service the rails and the trains. Each fifty miles of track meant the railroad had to put up a town. Some lasted, most didn't.

Idly, Spur wondered what the country and the town would look like in a hundred years, say 1971. He pondered on it a moment, shrugged and moved on. He had enough to worry about with the present, let alone the future.

He had not been thinking Indians. When he saw rail tracks he just discounted the idea of Indians being around, but he knew that was an over simplification.

There could be Oglala, Arapaho and Cheyenne in the area. It was mainly Cheyenne territory, but the other tribes were wandering more and more these days with all the white settlers surging into what were once reserved Indian hunting grounds.

A half hour later he had left the northern edges of Laramie far behind and was approaching the Circle

S ranch lands. He found a small rise and stared
ahead into the vast territory controlled by the Circle
S.

He could see no men riding guard duty. He sniffed
carefully but could detect no hint of wood smoke.
McCoy ground-tied his roan, sat down in the green
grass near the river and watched the water. Soon he
stretched out for a quick nap.

When he woke he sat up quickly. It was deep
dusk, and would be fully dark in another ten
minutes. Spur rode north. Once on the Circle S
lands, he moved cautiously, but saw nor heard any
riders.

Two-thirds of the way to the ranch house he heard
cattle. He didn't have to wonder what caused the
sounds. Spur had been on enough cattle trail drives
to recognize the clues. The lowing and bawling came
from a sizeable herd being contained and circled and
bedded down for the night.

Hopefully.

The toughest job a cowboy has to do is try to bed
down and control a herd that is not tired out, and
has a touch of spookiness about it. This herd seemed
to be of that type.

He found them just over a small hump of land to
the left. Spur sat his roan near the river and saw that
the cowboys had used the treeline as one boundary
and were herding the critters into a semblance of a
circle for the night. They were late. The bedding
down should have been done well before dark.

Spur watched them a moment. The beef obviously
were Circle S cattle that the new owner had decided
to sell. He remembered what the cattle buyer had
said and Rutger Shuntington's immediate anger at
the idea.

This was one herd that would never reach the rail
line. Spur moved back a quarter of a mile, dis-

mounted and cut the dynamite fuse he had brought into six-inch lengths and made a dozen bombs by pushing the detonator cap into a hole in the stick of powder, and inserting the burnable fuse into the hollow on the other end of the cap. The burning fuse had enough punch to set off the delicate dynamite detonator and that in turn exploded the powder.

Spur tested one of the sulphur matches he had in a packet and lit a piece of six-inch long fuse. It burned for a slow count of thirty. Most dynamite fuse burned a foot a minute, but some kinds went a lot faster than that. It paid to know which kind of fuse you were using.

Spur carried ten of the dynamite bombs inside his shirt, and two in his hands. He rode up near the herd in the thick darkness, dismounted and studied the cattle. Many were still up, turning, lowing, trying to move. Others had bedded down. A kind of nervous excitement seemed to run through the steers, cows and heifers.

It was a motley gathering, looking more like a roundup herd than a drive to the stockyards. But why else would there be a herd this size so close to the edge of the ranch and headed toward town?

Spur made up his mind. He left his horse and crawled as close to the herd as he felt he could get without being seen. He was still thirty yards from the stock. Then he waited for the night herder to make his round on horseback.

When the horseman was out of sight, Spur lit two fuses and threw the twin bombs within twenty feet of the steers. Then he pulled back and circled around the herd for fifty yards and started to light another fuse.

The first two dynamite bombs went off with a cracking roar that stick powder exploding in the open produces. At once the herd of about two-thousand cattle came on its feet, lowing and bawling. Spur bit the next fuse in half, lit it and threw the bomb.

He pitched four more of the short fused bombs before the next one exploded.

Now he pulled his six gun and began firing over the heads of the confused and frightened animals.

As the last of the bombs exploded, the whole herd began rushing away from the sound, away from the expected danger.

The cattle stampeded into the small camp the drovers had put up. In a few seconds hundreds of cattle had pushed over a chuck wagon, trampled the supplies into mush, destroyed everything in their path as they stampeded away from the danger.

Spur watched them go. Most of them wouldn't stop running for an hour. They would spread out in half a circle from the danger and it would take the poorly trained cow hands three or four days to find them all again in the plains and gullies of southern Wyoming.

Spur grinned as he watched.

But soon his grin faded. He heard riders coming toward him. A man shouted as if he were a cavalry sergeant, and the men on horseback seemed to be following his orders. What kind of a bunch of range hands were these, anyway?

Spur found his horse, jumped on board and whirled just as one of the riders spotted him.

The U.S. Secret Agent sat rock still on his mount as the lone rider bore down on him. At thirty yards, Spur lifted his six-gun and pounded off two quick shots. The close-by rider screamed as he jolted backwards off the saddle and rolled into a broken, dead mass of bones and flesh as he hit the ground.

Spur whirled his roan and raced away to the west. He heard shouted commands behind him and the riders seemed to track him to the west. He stopped and listened. At least four riders were coming his way.

He walked his gelding silently at right angles to
his former line of flight, now heading due south.

It took the Circle S riders three or four minutes to
pound across the prairie toward him. By that time
Spur had covered nearly a hundred yards south and
melted into the maw of the skinny moon darkness.

An outrider to the main force took Spur by surprise. The first he knew of the enemy was a blast of a
.44 and the whistling of hot lead past his shoulder.
Spur spun, his big .44 tracking the hard riding cowboy. The man had flattened out along the neck of his
horse to leave a smaller target.

Spur fired once and the cowboy screeched. The
round had slammed into his hip, half unseating him.
He dropped his six-gun and swore as he whipped his
mount around and charged away from Spur.

McCoy rode hard to the south now, depending on
the gelding's good lungs and strong legs to move
him away from the Circle S men. They would know
exactly where he was by the gunshots. It was run or
be overwhelmed.

Twenty minutes of hard riding and Spur could feel
the sweat and foam on the big gelding. A moment
later he saw the lights of Laramie. He doubted if the
Circle S riders would chase him all the way into the
little town. Spur stopped and listened. He could
hear no hoofbeats behind him. The closest saloon
was easy to hear, however. First there was laughter
and yelps of pleasure, then the deadly ring of a
pistol round and a lot of quiet following it.

Another typical night in a wild railroad town.

Spur looked for Rutger in his hotel room but the
room stood empty. The saloons were the next best
choice. After checking in four, Spur at last found
Rutger Shuntington confronting Elliot Parker.
Both men had been drinking, but neither was drunk.

McCoy pushed through the crowd and stood near the men but neither looked at him.

"Then you don't deny it?" Rutger challenged.

"I took what she offered. I did not force myself on her. I don't need to do that with any woman."

There were cheers and cat calls from the crowd of men.

"And I say you raped her! If you're any kind of a man at all you'll belt on a gun and meet me outside in five minutes. If you're not out there, I'll hunt you down like the raping, mad dog that you are!"

Rutger turned and downed the last of his whiskey, then walked out the door. A pistol came up by an unseen hand near Spur and the secret agent's fist slashed down where the gunman's wrist should be. It hit flesh and there was a crack as bones snapped.

A Circle S rider screeched, dropped his six-gun and bellowed in pain about his broken wrist. The crowd parted enough to show who the man was holding his broken wrist. Spur plowed his left fist into the cowboy's belly and when he bent over with the sudden new pain, Spur's right knee rammed upward into the man's chin snapping his head back. He crashed to the floor to the rear and Spur hurried out the door after Rutger.

The son of the former owner of the Circle S stood with his back against the ship lap siding of the hardware store watching everyone. He saw Spur and nodded.

"This is a strange place to find you after we decided you should stay out of sight for a few days."

"The bastard raped Priscilla a half hour after she got off the train. He's wanted her for years. I couldn't just stand by."

"Guess not. But you know it's dark out. In five minutes there'll be ten hidden Circle S guns waiting for you out here. All Parker has to do is walk out of a saloon door, draw his gun and you'll have ten rounds in you from ambush.''

''Dumb, all right. What I did was dumb. What's next?''

''Something smart. All we have to do is figure out something smart.''

''But I *am* meeting him. Not a chance I'll back down on this!''

''I was afraid you'd say something like that. I saw Priscilla a few hours ago. She did not look in dire straights to me.''

''She was covering it up.''

''So what do we do smart?''

Rutger shrugged. ''First, get off the street. Then you come up with an idea. You're the gunman.''

Spur nodded and they walked quickly back toward the hotel.

''There's a lightning struck cottonwood a half mile out of town north. I'll try to get Parker to be there in half an hour. We'll go out early and wait. We'll walk. You have a gun?''

Rutger patted his holster.

Spur found Parker still at the saloon bar where he had left him. He was about to take another whiskey when Spur knocked it off the bar.

''No time for that, Parker. I'm second for Rutger. He's calling you out at the lightning struck tree a half mile north of town. You be there in half an hour or ride out of town. You savvy?''

Parker stared at him. His eyebrows lifted, then his mouth twisted. ''Why the hell not? I used to be pretty good with a six-gun. I even have one in my office. Half an hour, I'll be there.''

As Spur turned he came face to face with Blade Gunnison. The five-foot, four-inch killer had to look up to see the lawman's face. Before he could even reach for his weapon, Spur's Colt was out and tapping the bad-ass on the chest.

"If I see you anywhere around this shootout, you'll be dead meat waiting for the buzzards tomorrow morning. You understand me?"

Gunnison blanched from embarrassment, slowly nodded, then reached up and brushed the muzzle off his chest.

"Hell yes, you I can get anytime, anytime at all."

Spur's eyes hooded. "No, small gunman, not anytime. You've missed at least four times in the past. Your next try will be your last one, so make it good. I'll be ready."

Spur kept his weapon out as he backed toward the door. He slammed through it and darted to one side. As he did he heard the roar of a six-gun behind him and lead smash into the wooden batwing door as it swung back in place.

Rutger was waiting for Spur in the alley next to the Medicine Bow Hotel and they used an Indian trot to move north to the old cottonwood.

"Indians can run at this pace for six hours without stopping and be ready to fight when they get there," Spur said.

Rutger panted like a steam engine on a siding. "Then they're in much better condition than I am."

They got to the old cottonwood and Spur told Rutger to stand behind it and not move until Parker came, no matter what happened.

"You expect visitors?"

"Yes, two or three to help out Parker. He might not even know about it."

Spur vanished into the darkness moving back toward town fifty yards. Spur wished he'd brought a rope, but that good idea came a little too late. He heard a horse coming down the trail.

The odds were that the man would stop short of the tree. Spur stood near the river behind some brush as the hoofbeats came closer. Then the mount angled into the brush where Spur stood. He waited

until the last possible split second, then jumped out
as the rider walked the horse past Spur.

Spur caught the rider's right arm and jerked him
off the horse.

"What the hell?" was all the man could say before
Spur slammed his .44 down hard on the black hatted
head. The bushwhacker crumpled and Spur tied his
hands and feet, then used the rider's neckerchief to
gag him.

Spur caught the horse, mounted it and found a
lariat hung around the horn. He shook it out, formed
a loop. It was a good rope. He nosed the black mare
out to the trail and waited. Three or four minutes
later a man rode hard for the big tree, pulled up
when he made it just past Spur and angled into a
patch of small cottonwoods on the other side of the
trail.

Spur dismounted, took the rope and worked
across the trail and through the woods. He spotted
the man checking a rifle and looking for a good field
of fire at the cottonwood.

McCoy formed a loop in the rope and twirled it, hit
a small tree and trailed the loop as he moved toward
his prey. In an open spot, the bushwhacker found a
downed log to fire over. The same opening also gave
Spur room to throw his loop and after two circles
over his head, he threw the rope and saw it settle
neatly over the rifleman.

Spur jerked backward with the rope wrapped
around both arms, and the gunman spilled into the
dirt, lost his rifle and found his arms pinned tightly
against his sides.

It took Spur only a moment to relax the pressure
on the rope. He darted forward twenty feet and
rammed one foot down on the gunman's chest.

"Well shuck my hide, look what I caught in my
loop," Spur drawled.

"Let me out of here!"

"Afraid not, bushwhacker. You was aiming to do a bad thing. Grown men been known to get themselves killed for trying what you're getting ready to try. You also ready to die, stranger?"

The man shrugged. "Shit yes. Been ready since the Wilderness."

"So you were in the war?"

"Hell, yes. Most men our age was in the war."

"And now you work for Curt Cameron. I've heard he's not really a rancher, true?"

The man laughed. "I might get sloppy on assignments like this, but I don't run off at the mouth. Forget it."

Spur put more pressure on his boot until the man wheezed.

"Go ahead, stomp me. Told you I was ready. One way or another, don't matter a damn bit to me."

The secret agent growled and tied up the man with the rope and made sure his horse was tied. Then he gagged the man and went back to the trail.

Ten minutes later, another rider came up the trail, his horse at a walk. He sat upright, his left hand holding the reins and his right on his six-gun on his right hip. He stared at the brush on both sides.

Spur let him pass. The man was Elliot Parker. Spur followed him on foot. Parker got to the old cottonwood and dismounted, drew his gun a few times and then looked around.

"I'm here, Rutger, where the hell are you?"

Spur moved around through the brush until he could see Rutger, then he slid up beside him without a sound.

"Oh God! you scared me!" Rutger whispered.

"It's time. If you're determined."

"I've got to. I made a public call out. He raped Priscilla. There's no other way."

Spur sighed. "All right. You have six rounds in your weapon?"

"No. Oh, sure, I might need them. I'm not what you'd mistake for a crack shot."

Rutger took a round from his belt and pushed it in the empty chamber, then let the hammer down cautiously on the round. He straightened his shoulders. He walked out from the cottonwood.

Parker stood thirty feet away.

"Parker, you rapist! Are you ready to apologize to Priscilla and stand trial for rape?"

Parker whirled, his hand on his gun. He saw in the sliver of moonlight that Rutger had not drawn.

"Not guilty. Sure she protested a little, they all do the first few times. Or are you still a virgin yourself, Shuntington?"

Rutger drew his six-gun and fired. He didn't aim, it was an automatic reaction. Then he shivered, lifted the weapon and tried to aim at the other man.

Parker had been jolted by the shot and drew as fast as he could. He hadn't fired a pistol in two years. Now he stood facing Rutger, his feet spread wide. Too late he realized he made a larger target that way.

Then Rutger walked deliberately forward. He fired twice more and missed.

Parker fired once and the round hit the ground ten feet in front of him. He swore and tried to aim. He fired again and missed.

Then in a hazy, dark scene, Parker realized that Rutger was running, running straight at him! The Shuntington pistol fired again and again, but missed. Parker wanted to turn and run, but he couldn't. He couldn't even move. He hated death more than anything, and now he stared at it in the face of a twenty-one year old angry young man!

Rutger counted his rounds. He had fired five times. He had one round left. He ran faster, saw Parker frozen in place and this time he lifted his arm higher, pointed his whole arm at Parker's chest and fired.

If he missed he was dead, because Parker must have three or four rounds left.

The old Remington pistol belched smoke and sound and sent a .44 round spiraling toward its target. The lead shattered the fourth button on Elliot Parker's shirt front, blasted through skin and tissue, sliced through the far side of one lung and chopped up a dozen medium sized arteries before it lodged near his spine.

Parker felt the blow in his chest, dropped his own gun and staggered backward from the force of the heavy slug. He sat down, then fell on his back and to his surprise found that he couldn't roll over or even try to get up.

His chest felt warm, but it didn't hurt. He couldn't have been hit badly. His arms wouldn't move. He lifted his head and saw Rutger walking toward him. Then the other man, the one from the saloon came up. The two talked a moment, then one kicked away Parker's gun and they squatted beside him.

Parker felt fingers open his shirt, then dark eyes winced and head shook.

"Parker, you're hit bad, almost gut shot. Can you move?"

"No," Parker said, surprised that he could still talk. "Guess I ain't dead yet."

"Not yet," Spur said.

"But soon, right?" Parker asked.

"Be my guess," McCoy said.

"Tell us about the ranch," Rutger said.

"I helped on the papers, the legal work. Hell, this guy comes in one day and says I can be one-third owner of the Circle S within a month. That had to be thirty, forty-thousand dollars for me! A fortune! I never make more than about five-hundred a year."

Parker coughed, spit some blood out on his white shirt, but didn't notice it.

"Hell, I took the deal. I fixed up the papers, they come back all signed and looked legal. I never asked how this Cameron arranged it."

"Murder and forgery, most likely," Spur said.

"I got five-thousand cash," Parker said. He coughed again and almost couldn't stop. More blood came out.

"The money is all in my desk drawer. Couldn't put it in the bank, that would cause suspicion. It's there. Guess I owe it to Priscilla and Rutger here. Damn, I'll never spend a dollar of it!"

He wheezed a moment.

"What happened to Rutger's mother and father out at the ranch, and the 35 to 45 ranch hands?"

"Not sure, just some hints. My guess is that. . . ." This time when Parker coughed he never stopped. Blood spouted from his mouth and then he sighed and his head turned to one side.

"Dead," Spur said.

They tied the lawyer over his saddle and headed back for town. On the way Spur untied the two Circle S riders he had bound before.

"You show your face in town again, I'll kill you!" Spur bristled at them. "You get on those nags and you ride for Cheyenne and don't ever come back here again!"

Both men nodded and rode out hard to the east.

"Come on, Rutger. We know part of the story about what happened to your ranch. Now we have to find out the rest of it."

9

Even though it was dark when they walked the lawyer's horse back to town that night, a trail of curious people followed them to the sheriff's office.

The people could tell the man was dead, but they couldn't see who it was, and neither Spur nor Rutger said a word.

At the sheriff's office, Spur stayed with the body as Rutger went inside and came back with the law man. The thin faced man lit his pipe as he walked, checked the face of the corpse and straightened.

"All right, people," Sheriff Dryer boomed. "This body is our former town lawyer, Elliot Parker. He came upon some misfortune. Now everybody get out of here, nothing more to look at. Scoot! All of you, unless you want to spend a night rent free in county jail!"

The crowd of about twenty people slowly faded away, but new faces came to take their places.

"Tell me about it tomorrow," Sheriff Dryer said to Spur. "I'll get his bones down to the undertaker and out of sight. Hear you sent two Circle S crooks down the trail. Good. Watch your hindside. Still a batch of gunmen in town."

Spur and Rutger went part way with the body, ducked into an alley and soon made their way by alleys and side streets to the back door of lawyer Elliot Parker's office. Spur held up the keys he had removed from the legal man's body. He found the one to fit the rear door and they slipped inside.

Neither man said a word. Spur waved Rutger forward. He walked to the big desk and pulled out drawers until he found an envelope and a leather bag. The envelope had a stack of fifty dollar bills in it, and the bag contained twenty dollar-gold pieces.

"Must be it," Spur said. We can count it later. Should be five-thousand dollars there. You want me to keep it for you?"

"Most of it," Rutger said. He took out four of the fifty dollar bills and they went out the back door. No light had shown inside the office, no one would know they had been there.

"It ain't like we're stealing," Rutger protested without any cause. "I'm just getting back what's legal and by rights, mine."

"Agreed," Spur said.

They kept to the alleys until they came to the side door of the Medicine Bow Hotel. Upstairs, Priscilla opened her door when she recognized Rutger's voice. She threw her arms around his, tears of joy in her eyes.

"I was terrified! I thought for certain he'd kill you. You were never any good with a six-gun. Remember when daddy finally let me learn to shoot and I beat you that time."

Rutger grinned and ushered Priscilla inside her room. "I'll sleep on the floor here tonight, and Mr. McCoy will be right next door. I don't think anybody is going to be after us, but you never can tell.

That night no one tried to get in either room.

The next morning, Rutger hired a guard to sit in front of Priscilla's door with a shotgun loaded with double-ought buck rounds. The extra long shells had thirteen .32 caliber slugs in each load and would blow a grown man in half at twenty feet.

Spur sat outside the side door of the bank early, the next morning and as soon as Ira Villary unlocked the door, Spur asked if he could come inside.

"You have those new fangled lock boxes a person can rent and lock up in your safe?"

"Indeed we do, Mr. McCoy. We call them safe deposit boxes. New York started them six years ago, so we're not far behind them. We have two sizes." He looked at the leather bag Spur took out of a folded copy of the newspaper.

"I'd say you'll need the large size. Rents for six dollars a year . . . unless this is official business of the U.S. Government."

"We're told to pay our way, Mr. Villary. Be glad to pay. Just set it up now, I've got some rather pressing business to take care of."

Villary made out a form, had Spur sign it, then smiled. "Hear you were involved in bringing in a dead body last night."

"True," McCoy said.

"Hear it was Elliot Parker."

"Right. He was involved with the takeover of the Shuntington ranch, but don't tell anyone."

Spur took the key Villary gave to him, put it on a new pocket watch chain and key ring, and dropped it into his pocket. "Thanks for accommodating me before banking hours, Mr. Villary."

"Oh, quite all right. In a small town, the bank is open whenever I'm here. Common courtesy to my friends."

Spur left quickly, had a fast stack of hot cakes smothered with four sunnyside-up eggs and six slices of sausage. What he needed now was more information.

A hour hour later, Spur sat on his roan a quarter of a mile north of town on the trail that led to the

Circle S ranch. He figured there would be a messenger or a pair of Circle S riders coming to town this morning.

By eight-thirty he found out he was half right. One rider with a new Circle S brand on his sorrel's hip rode out from town and headed for the ranch. He looked like he had been through a rough night with a pair of large bottles and a tireless woman.

Spur waited until the rider hit the fringe of trees where it was darker and sent a round from his pistol over the cowboy's head.

"Stand and deliver!" Spur bellowed. The traditional call of the robber and highwayman had the desired effect. The cowboy meekly raised his hands.

"Ain't got but a fifty-cent piece on me, stranger," the cowboy said. "That whore Vetta she done me out of every last dollar I had and woulda got the rest 'ceptin she missed it. She was half as drunk as I was, reckon."

"Get down, my side, and drop your iron in the dust. Move slow or you're dinner for some turkey buzzard."

The man moved cautiously, and soon had dropped his weapon and stood on the ground.

"Now, unbelt your pants and let them down to your ankles," Spur demanded.

"What'n hell?"

"Drop your pants, now!" Spur roared.

The cowboy shrugged, let his pants fall down and it became evident he wore no underwear.

Spur eased out of his saddle. He looped the bridle rein over the roan's head so it fell to the ground. The horse was ground-tied and wouldn't move more than a foot or two.

"You work the Circle S?" Spur asked.

"Yeah."

"You don't seem to be much of a cowboy."

"Ain't one, usual."

"What are you, usually?"

"Can't say."

Spur drew his Colt .44 smoothly, fast and put a slug between the rider's feet. The round cut through two layers of pants where they had fallen.

"Hey!"

"I asked what you do regular?"

The rider didn't answer.

"I can start putting a slug in your knee caps until you remember," Spur said.

"Cripple me?"

"Before I kill you. If you won't talk, what good are you to me?"

"You kill me I never can talk," the rider said smugly.

Spur slammed his fist into the rider's nose which erupted with a gush of blood that ran down his mouth and dripped off his chin.

"Goddamn!"

"What's your usual occupation?"

"Ain't done much since the war. I was a corporal."

"For the south?"

"Yes sir. Hell, most men our age was in the big war. Bet you was yourself."

"What is Curt Cameron? He sure isn't a rancher."

"Can't say."

Spur shot him in the shoulder. The heavy slug jolted through flesh, missed the bone, but slammed the rider backwards three feet and dropped him on his knees.

"You bastard! You shot me!"

"Soldiers get shot all the time. You've been shot before. I asked you who your boss is. He's no cattleman. He took over the ranch illegally by using forged deeds and bills of sale. Where does he come from and what's his racket here?"

"He'd kill me, sure."

"Maybe, if he found out. I'm the one who will kill you for sure, and I'm running out of time."

One of the horses skittered to one side and Spur looked up to find a three-foot long rattlesnake slithering away from the mount's hind feet. Spur grabbed a stick and caught up with the big diamondback and held its head to the ground with the stick.

He grabbed the writhing creature directly behind the triangular shaped head and carried it back to where the Circle S man stood ground tied by his trousers around his ankles.

"I hear you southern boys like to milk rattlesnakes like this frisky little critter," Spur said, waving the hissing snake a foot from the rider.

The man stumbled backward.

"Get that damned thing away from me!"

Spur grinned. "What, you don't like rattlers? He's going to be in your pocket for the rest of our little chat, you'll get to be good friends—if he doesn't bite you too many times. I've heard the average man can take two rattler bites, but after that he's bound to be dead before long. It's the swelling and the burning that's the most painful, they say, but one or two fang punctures isn't so bad."

The cowboy's face had paled to flour white.

"What's your name?" Spur barked at him.

"Seth Felson." The word came softly.

"You work for Curt Cameron?"

"Yes sir."

"He runs some kind of outlaw gang?"

"Yes sir."

"And you're stealing the Shuntington ranch from its lawful owners?"

"We did, yes."

Spur moved the snake closer. "The couple that

lived there, the Shuntingtons. What happened to them?"

"Swear I don't know. They was gone when I rode in. A dozen of us come in late. We had . . . had another job we was on. Curt said it was all right."

"You ever see fresh graves around the farmyard?"

"No sir. Don't know what happened to them."

"What about the crew? Thirty-five men just vanished. Where did they go to?"

"They was all gone, too, when I rode in."

Spur pushed the diamondback up until its darting tongue almost touched the hated human animal. Seth stumbled backward and sat down hard when he tripped over his dropped pants. He held his shoulder and blood seeped through his fingers.

Spur knelt in front of him still holding the snake.

"Why is Curt selling off the cattle?"

"We always do. I guess he wants the money. Cattle are hard to spend."

"What happens when you sell off all the cattle?"

"Curt sells the ranch and we move on."

"To another ranch where you kill the owners, forge the papers and take over the spread?"

"Hell, I don't know. It's all done before most of us get there. The Captain knows what he's doing. He treats us right."

"Captain?"

"He . . . he must have been an officer in the war."

"But you still call him Captain?"

"Yeah . . . so what?"

"You have sergeants, too?"

"Course not. We ain't in the army no more."

"Everyone in your gang was in the Rebel army?"

"Hell, I don't know . . . some of them."

Spur used a length of rawhide and tied it around a stake, then drove the stake in the ground. He tied the other end of the three foot rawhide strip to the tail of the snake. The reptile hissed and crawled away from them as far as it could.

"What you doing?"

Spur whittled two more stakes sharp and pounded them into the ground with a rock. Then he tied one of Fesler's wrists to the stake and reached for the other one. The outlaw jerked his hand away.

"You tying me here? What if that diamondback comes this way?"

"Spit in his eye. Hear diamondback rattlers hate that."

"He'll kill me, sure as hell! That's a damn mad snake!"

"Tell me what happened to the ranch owners and the crew."

"Christ! I would if I knew. Curt, he don't tell his men everything. He says we don't need to know. He says what we don't know, we can't tell."

"Like now," Spur said. "Only that way you wind up getting yourself killed, slowly."

"Christ sakes. I told you all I know."

"You've done this ranch stealing before?"

Fesler hesitated. "Yeah. Three or four times, takes six months sometimes. This one was gonna be quicker. Curt, he wants to get to St. Louis and meet this woman. . . ."

Spur reached down and sliced the rawhide with his knife. It had a six inch blade, honed sharp enough to cut hair.

"Pull up your pants."

"Thanks."

When Seth Fesler had his pants up and buttoned, he looked at Spur.

"Take out all but five rounds from your gunbelt loops."

"What?"

"Pull out the rounds and give them to me. Now!"

Seth did as directed. Spur walked over and picked

up the man's six-gun, drained out the live rounds, caught them and put them in his pocket. Spur checked the man's saddle. He had no rifle. In the saddlebags were chewing tobacco and a pint of whiskey. Nothing else.

"Fesler, you want to live to see the noonday sun?"

"Damn right!"

"You just resigned from Curt Cameron's outfit. You quit his little army, you understand?"

"I guess."

"You damn well better. I'm going to take him down, and his gang. Half of them are going to hang. You'll be first on my list if I find you out at the ranch when we take it. You get on that nag, turn her head west and ride the tracks for fifty miles and you'll come to a train town."

"You want me to run?"

"Damn right, Fesler. Run or die. Take your pick."

"I'm running. I get my iron?"

Spur tossed him the empty weapon. "Don't load it until you're ten miles from here. I see that weasel-ugly face of yours again, I'll put two .44 slugs into it. Now ride!"

Spur watched the man run to his horse, flip up the reins and mount, then spur the animal due west with a slight angle south to pick up the Union Pacific tracks.

Spur nodded grimly as the outlaw rode away. He threw rocks into the Laramie river and scowled at the ripples. Something still didn't ring true. How could Curt Cameron have such a vice-like hold on so many men? And they called him Captain. So maybe some of them had even served with him in gray uniforms during the war.

The fight had been over for six years! How could Curt hold them together for one swindle like this every six months? Of course, if they cleared enough money . . . If they sold five-thousand head of steer at twenty-dollars each that would be...He hesitated. A hundred-thousand dollars! Enough to keep forty men loyal for a while.

Spur rode back toward town trying to fill in the pieces of the puzzle. The biggest was what happened to the ranch owners and the thirty-five members of the crew. Men didn't just vanish into thin air, not even in Wyoming.

Curt Cameron looked out across the ranch from the bedroom window. It would take them three days to round up the cattle that someone spooked last night. It had to be Spur McCoy. Why wouldn't he die?

The dynamite charges and the pistol shots had spooked an already nervous bunch of cattle. His men had not been able to hold them and some had run twenty miles before they stopped. Now he had to rely on the best cowmen in his group, and there weren't many of them.

Real cowboys could do the job in a day and a half. It might take his men four or five days.

Damnit! That meant four or five days more until he could sell the first batch of two-thousand head. Then he'd have to do another roundup. Why was this one being so difficult, so damned hard?

He knew at once. Spur McCoy. He had increased the price on the man's head, but none of his hotshots in town had come with the man's topknot in a bucket. Curt snorted. He might have to ride into town and take care of the matter himself.

His basic plan still held. He would sell off every available steer and half to three-quarters of the breeding stock. He'd strip the place and try to come up with five or six-thousand head of cattle to market. Then he'd sell the real estate for ten or fifteen thousand, whatever the market would allow, and they would ride out of there for a long break in

St. Louis. Yeah, and he'd see Wanda again!

Just thinking about her gave him a hot feeling.

But before Wanda, they would put a new twist to this one. They could not simply ride away innocent as doves this time. That damned McCoy made it impossible. And the owner's son and daughter had complicated it beyond belief.

Now he heard that the lawyer, Elliot Parker, had got himself killed over the girl by her brother. Damn fool. He was in line to clear ten to fifteen-thousand dollars. He'd been worth it.

So the situation had changed. After they sold the ranch, they would sweep into town, clean out the bank, rob every store in sight, gun down the sheriff and anybody else who objected, and ride out with more cash money than his men had ever seen before!

Hell, they would also stop the train outside of town and blow open the express car safe and see if any gold was going out to the mint in San Francisco! They might pick up another twenty, thirty-thousand in gold bullion!

Damn, he was getting a hard-on, just thinking about it.

"Lucia! Lucia you tight little twat, get in here!" He bellowed it once more and she slid around the doorframe with her blouse half open and wearing nothing under it.

"You called me, big daddy dick?"

Shit! she did get his fires burning hot.

"Take that blouse off, now!" he said, his voice growing thick with emotion and desire. Christ, she knew how to get him worked up.

The blouse slid off her arms and she turned, letting one breast after the other swing out toward him. She shook her shoulders slowly making her twin peaks jiggle and bounce and swing in small circles.

She stayed barely out of his reach. At last he

lunged out, grabbed one breast and pulled her to
him. He caught her other pink-tipped breast in his
mouth and munched on it until she groaned with her
own desire.

She pushed away from where they stood by the
big bed. Slowly she slid down her skirt and he
watched in amazement. She wore nothing under the
heavy skirt. Not a fucking thing!

Curt growled, grabbed her naked body and threw
it on the bed. Then he leaped on top of her writhing
form.

She laughed and squealed as she pulled his clothes
off. When he was naked she turned soft and gentle,
stroking his penis, cupping his heavy balls, rubbing
her breasts across his chest until he wailed and
spread her legs.

"Damn, but you know how to get me moving. You
sure you've never been a whore in some saloon?"

"You taught me everything I know about
fucking!" she whispered in his ear. "You sweet cock,
that's why I'm so fucking good at it!"

He wailed in delight, dropped between her legs
and in one swift, searing stroke lanced into her.

Lucia screeched in sudden pain, then was lost in
the rapture at the end of the stroke and the delight
of his presence. She gripped him with her muscles
and stroked him as he plunged forward, thinking
now only of his own need and his urgency.

He was always so damn fast. Once a day satisfied
him. She usually found one of the men who could
treat her soft and gentle the way a lady should be
treated. Then she demanded her own pleasure first,
and if the man could last, he would get his chance to
enter her. Ladies first, she told them, and they were
so glad just to see her naked that it worked every
time. If Curt knew, he said nothing. He was getting
more than he could handle as it was.

She smiled at the man over her plunging and

snorting, sweating and rutting at her. Once they got back to St. Louis she had promised herself it would be payoff time. Curt didn't know it but she had found one of his bank passbooks and could forge his name perfectly.

Once in St. Louis she would get everything she could from him and vanish down the Mississippi on a river boat. Back to New Orleans where the living was easy—especially with fifteen or twenty-thousand dollars he had in that one account.

Lucia encouraged him to climax quickly, knowing he would roll away then at once, his mind on new matters, his loins drained, and his brain busy with some new swindle.

Just wait until St. Louis, Curt Cameron! Then they would find out who was the best swindler after all. Lucia had no doubt who would win on that score. She had ways, and she had the fucking little passbook that was the answer to all of her dreams for the rest of her life!

10

The sun stood directly overhead when Spur rode back into town after counseling with the Circle S hand and his pet rattlesnake. He had cut the rawhide off the critter and let it slither away into the brush. That was the snake's home range and he had a perfect right to be there.

Spur came into town from the east, rode down the alley to the back door of the jail and slid inside. He knew that several of the Circle S men were still in town hunting him. They had been more cautious lately since several of them had wound up in boot hill under six-feet of Wyoming soil.

Sheriff Dryer grunted when he saw Spur.

"How the hell is the United States Secret Service doing on our case?"

Spur laughed and dropped into the captain's chair beside the sheriff's scarred desk.

"Better than expected, Sheriff Dryer. But not as good as hoped for. From what the lawyer told us, and what I've just gleaned from a reluctant Circle S witness staring eyeball to eyeball with a diamond-back rattler, this outfit is an outlaw gang, straight and simple."

"But we can't arrest them without some proof."

"True, but we can harass the hell out of them and

118

hope they show their hand, or play the wrong card."

"I don't follow you."

"The boss of this gang moves in, takes over a ranch, then he sells off all the cattle he can, sells the ranch at a bargain price and moves on. The whole thing looks legitimate. It stands that way unless somebody can prove the takeover was a fraud or swindle or done with the help of murder and forgery."

"Yeah, but we got to prove it."

"Not if we get them scared, make them do something stupid so we'll have the break we need."

"How can we do that?"

"I'm working on it."

"You say they plan on stripping the spread of all the steers and probably most of the breeding stock?"

"Been the pattern in the past," Spur said.

"So maybe we can slow down the sales."

"They've already contacted a buyer. I stampeded about two-thousand head last night, so it'll take them a day or two to round them up."

"So what good is a day or two?"

"We try to make them nervous. Is there another lawyer in town?"

"One more. He's not all that good."

"Doesn't matter, I know the law well enough. We're going to have Rutger Shuntington challenge the sale of the ranch, challenge the signature on the grant deed and on the bill of sale. We'll declare both to be forgeries and try to get the assets of the ranch tied up in a lawsuit. Then Cameron can't sell the cattle."

Sheriff Dryer shook his head. "Nice plan . . ." He sucked on his pipe and blew out a blue cloud of smoke, "But it won't work. Circuit court judge was through town last week, and he won't be back for a month. Could take the train to Cheyenne and get a

special court order, that would take three to four
weeks for all the legal mumbo jumbo. Sorry."

Spur paced the office, hands behind his back, his
scowl firmly in place.

"Damn! So we try something else." He grinned
and dropped into the chair. "So we do it home grown
style. From what I hear there has been a hell of a lot
of cattle rustling going on in this county lately. And
as sheriff, it's your responsibility to see that none of
those cattle get sold and out of state before you
inspect them."

Sheriff Dryer laughed. "And so I have to examine
every brand on every critter before it can be
shipped. Take two or three days for a big herd."

"Yeah, good thinking. And just maybe your
brand inspector is in Cheyenne at the funeral of a
close relative and won't be back for a week. He's the
best brand man in the state and you won't move on
clearing the herds until he checks them. Still you'll
get the job done just as fast as possible."

Sheriff Dryer grinned. "I think we've got a way to
hold up any cattle sale. The buyer will go along with
it. He's got more stock now than he really wants.
Nobody else around here has many steers to sell
anyway so we won't hurt the other ranchers."

Spur stood. "We have our stopper in place. Now I
want to get a lawsuit started, at least. We'll draw up
some legal looking papers and have them served on
the first Circle S rider you can find. Order him to
take them directly to Mr. Cameron or his ass will get
burned. It'll be another good scare for Mr. Cameron.
The more barbs we can jab him with, the more nervous he's going to get."

Spur went out the front door of the sheriff's office,
straight across the street and down a few doors to
Amy York's seamstress establishment. He hadn't
seen her for a few days, and she might have heard
some news he could use.

She smiled when he walked in. He saw that she
had on an attractive dress, and her hair was done up
in a new way.

"My, my, my, but you're looking just as pretty as
a bouncing long-haired kitten this afternoon, Amy."

She smiled. "Thank you, kind sir." She laughed
and her eyes traveled down his body, stopping at his
crotch. "You're looking extremely good yourself."

Before either of them could say another word, a
man burst through the front door pulling at a six-
gun in his holster. The trigger hung up or he would
have killed them both.

Spur drew his .44 smoothly and blasted a round
just as Blade Gunnison jerked out the weapon and
dodged to one side. The lead slug slammed into the
cylinder on the other weapon, smashing it out of
Blade's hand.

The short man charged Spur in a surprise move.
The two had been only eight-feet apart and before
Spur could fire again, Gunnison had jolted him
backwards, knocked the weapon from Spur's hand
and they fell over a clothes dummy and rolled on the
floor.

Spur was a head taller than the short, thickset
man, but the Circle S enforcer was tough as old
buffalo hide. He squirmed and kicked and dug his
elbow into Spur's midsection, then clawed at a six-
inch knife on his belt.

Spur got a hand lose and blasted a solid fist into
Blade's jaw jolting him to the side. They rolled on
the floor and Spur jumped up looking for his six-
gun. He had no hideout. The small man got out his
knife but Spur surprised him with a sudden kick
that slanted off Blade's wrist and spun the knife
away. It fell and stuck in the wooden floor.

Blade charged like a rampaging bull. He lowered
his head and bellowed as he stormed forward. Spur
had no place to dodge hemmed in on one side by

bolts of cloth and on the other by a sewing table.
Blade's strong, thick arms wrapped around Spur as
they slammed against the wall and slid to the floor.

Spur got his hand under Blade's chin and rammed
his head upward until the smaller man's eyes
bulged. Blade released the bear hug grip and his
fingers clawed for Spur's face. One fingernail drew a
bloody line down Spur's cheek but missed his eye.

Spur changed his hands on Blade's chin grabbing
his throat in a strangle hold. Just as he was
tightening it to cut off all breath to the man, Spur
felt Blade shift his position. Then his knee came
crashing upward, skidded off Spur's thigh and
barely touched Spur's scrotum before it smashed
into his belly.

McCoy could do little but hold on. A flood of
sudden pain and bile flooded his system. His
testicles felt crushed, but he knew they were only
grazed. A direct blow would have disabled him and
Blade would have killed him quickly.

The outlaw saw his advantage and pushed away
from Spur and scrambled to his feet. He darted to
his still quivering knife, jerked it from the floor and
sprang to the side grabbing Amy by one breast.

"You want me to slice her tit off?" the outlaw
demanded.

Spur rolled over and came to his feet. He looked
more threatening than he felt. His balls still ached,
sending wave after wave of nausea through his
system.

"No . . . this isn't her fight. Leave her out of it."

Blade waved the knife. "Move over there by the
wall, face it, hands high on the wall, your legs
spread." Blade's eyes searched the room looking for
Spur's gun. His own must be jammed. He'd seen a
pistol hit by a bullet before.

Spur watched him. If the outlaw found the gun,
both he and Amy were dead. He tried to get that

thought to her as he stared at her, but he wasn't sure she understood. She shivered, her hands at her side. Then Spur saw that she held a pair of big scissors she had been using. He looked down at them, then at her, then down at them again.

She understood.

"You'll never find my gun," Spur said sharply.

Blade looked up, uncertainty showing on his face.

"Now!" Spur bellowed.

Amy had changed her hand on the scissors, holding them now like a stabbing knife. She thrust the sharp points of the scissors upward. Spur saw she had closed her eyes. There was no way she could miss hitting the man standing directly in front of her.

As she moved, Spur blasted away from the wall, pushing with both hands and one foot. It all happened in a few seconds. Spur hurtled across the six-feet of space toward the pair. Amy's scissors flashed upward driven by desperation and fear. The point hit Blade's sagging belly, penetrated two inches and brought a scream of rage from the out-law.

By the time he realized he had been wounded and he reacted with the knife on Amy's breast, he was too late. McCoy was in front of him, his big fist hammering down on Blade's right wrist like a pile driver, smashing the bone, spinning the knife away harmlessly.

Spur followed through with a crashing left fist to Blade's jaw, driving him backwards away from Amy.

"Get outside!" Spur roared at Amy. She darted for the door, made it and ran outside screaming at the top of her voice, still carrying the bloody scissors.

"That bitch stuck me!" Blade bellowed. "You're a dead man, McCoy!"

The knife lay on the floor between them.

Blade looked at it. Spur saw the glance.

"Go ahead, try for it!" Spur said.

Blade hesitated. Spur got there first, his big boot slamming down on the blade, putting it out of the contest.

Blade ran for the front door. Spur could not get there in time to stop him. They both stormed into the street a moment later. Spur had only his own sheath knife on his belt.

He knew what Blade was looking for—a gun. Blade was ten-feet ahead when he spotted a cowboy with a gunbelt. He charged the man, grabbing at the six-gun. The cowboy lunged away from him and got free.

Blade came up behind another man with a gun-belt. He pulled the six-gun out of the holster before the victim knew Blade was behind him.

Blade turned with the gun coming up, his thumb dragging back the hammer to half cock. Spur knew he had to do something quickly. Ten feet!

He charged forward, digging at the snap on his sheath knife scabbard. The knife came out.

A pistol blasted from across the street. Spur felt the slug tear into his left shoulder at the same instant he heard the shot. That shot was followed by another from a distance, then he felt himself being driven to the left by the force of the heavy pistol round.

Directly in front of him the stolen pistol fired and he felt the hot breath of the round. The shot from across the street had saved his life. But for how long?

As he fell he used the fractions of a second to throw his knife. One turn, throw hard!

The six-inch knife spun once and the sharp blade drove into Gunnison's right biceps. Gunnison screamed. He dropped the gun. The cowboy who had lost his weapon grabbed Gunnison from behind in an arm lock around his throat and held the smaller man.

Spur fell and rolled trying to take the force of the ground on his right shoulder instead of the injured one. He came to his feet with the pain seeping from between clenched teeth. He had no weapon at all now. Through a haze of anger and agony, he saw Blade held tightly by the man behind him.

The next moment Blade jerked forward, threw the cowboy over his head and dumped him on the ground, then rushed down the street to an alley and ran into the darkness.

Spur picked up the dropped gun and charged after him. His left arm hung almost useless. He hoped the gun he held still had four rounds in it.

It was a short alley. Spur saw no one in it as he looked into the daylight shadows. He ran hard to the end of the building and peered around it. Blade jumped back behind a stack of wooden crates fifty-feet down the connecting alley near the hardware store's back door.

Spur walked forward slowly, a calm had dropped over him. He knew where the man was, the man deserved killing, Spur McCoy was going to do society's job.

Gunnison threw a two-by-four at Spur. The two-foot long missile landed short.

There were no handy weapons to steal back here. It was one-on-one and Spur had the borrowed .44.

"Give it up!" Spur bellowed. "You come out now with your hands pushing sky and you get to live to stand trial."

"No damned trial!" Gunnison screeched.

Spur saw him two rungs up a ladder, nailed to the side of the building. His right arm was useless. It's tough to climb a vertical ladder with one hand, Spur knew.

"Down!" Spur demanded as he walked up to Gunnison.

"Don't shoot, damnit! I'm helpless. Bastard! I should have killed you six times!"

"But you missed. And there won't be a next time."

Gunnison hung there by his one hand, four-feet off the ground. He couldn't go up.

"Help me down."

Spur laughed. "Hell, you climbed up there, you can get down, hurt arm or no."

Spur heard something at the other end of the alley. It could be some of Gunnison's buddies. His shoulder throbbed where he had been shot. Blood oozed and dripped down his side staining his shirt. He glanced down the alley.

It had been what Blade had been waiting for. He pushed away from the ladder, his feet aimed at Spur's chest. One of his boots smashed the six-gun from Spur's hand, the other hit him in the chest and sprawled him backwards in the dust. Spur was on his feet before Gunnison.

They faced each other. Spur could only think of a weapon. What did he have? Not even a pen knife. In his shirt pocket he had a new lead pencil he had sharpened that morning in the Sheriff's office.

Yes! He pulled it out, put it between his two middle fingers after forming a fist. The eraser was against his palm and the point sticking six-inches out of the other side of his fist. All he had to do was keep the pencil straight with his forearm and he had a deadly weapon.

Blade laughed. "You gonna hurt me with a damn lead pencil?"

Spur didn't reply. He moved to his left. Gunnison moved the other way. They stood four-feet apart. Spur knew if the fight lasted much longer Gunnison's friends would find them. They all had six-guns and would use them with delight.

Spur dodged sharply to the left, then back to the right and then to the left again. The movement made his shot shoulder scream with pain, but Spur moved in spite of it.

He caught Gunnison trying to change directions. Spur sprang forward, lunging with all his two-hundred pounds behind his thrust with the pencil. His wounded left arm hung useless at his side. The pencil was firm and steady, straight out from his hand like an extension of his forearm.

Gunnison had time only to stare down at the sharp point as it slammed forward toward his chest. He twisted but the pencil point needled through his shirt, met flesh and won the battle.

The pencil plunged into Blade's chest, missed his heart but ruptured a big artery coming out of it.

Blade Gunnison fell backwards into the dust and horse droppings of the alley. He stared at Spur in shock, surprise and deadly disbelief.

"Can't be!" he rumbled. "Hell, can't be! I ain't gonna die from being hurt by a damn lead pencil!"

Spur had let go of the pencil when it impaled the outlaw. Now Gunnison touched the two-inches of the pencil that stuck out of his chest.

"Don't move it!" Spur said quickly.

"Hell, I know that much," Gunnison said. "You by god killed me with a fucking pencil!"

"Tell me about Curt Cameron. He was a Rebel Captain of cavalry in the war?"

"Yeah."

"And he got some of the men together to form an outlaw gang?"

"Shit yes! We done good for years."

"Until now." Spur watched his color fade as blood pumped from ruptured veins inside his body.

"What happened to the Shuntington's?"

"Damned if I know. One day they was there, and

the next day nobody heard nothing more about them. Left for back East, I hear."

"You know better. Tell me what happened. They're both dead, right?"

"You tell me. Men of the Twenty-Seventh don't talk out of school."

"What was that?"

Blade Gunnison smiled, shook his head and gave one long last gush of air from his dead lungs. His eyes stared at Spur, but they only saw eternity.

Spur lifted off the ground and walked down the alley to Dr. Asamore's office.

"Heard some shots, wondered if it would be good for business," the old doctor drawled with a grin.

"Not good on shoulders. How bad is it, Doc?"

"Tolerable. Tolerable that is for a body with as many scars and slashes and bullet holes in it as yours has. How many times you been shot?"

"Twenty, maybe, maybe twice that many. I lost count. It still hurts just as bad every time."

"You know about alcohol on an open wound then?"

"Yeah. Do it. I've still got work to get done."

Spur McCoy passed out when the alcohol hit the open flesh on his shoulder. The bullet had done more surface damage than internal. It slashed across the shoulder, bounced off the bone and angled down into the bicep and exited. Nasty, lots of blood but not totally debilitating.

A half hour later Spur sat in the sheriff's office.

"So it was you who saved my scalp this time," Spur said.

"Saw the Circle S man watching you come boiling out of the dress shop. He followed and gunned you before I could get there, so I put him down with a shot. Then I lost you."

The sheriff watched Spur a minute.

"You killed Blade Gunnison with a lead pencil?"

"A man can get desperate at times, Sheriff. Lots of common items can be used as weapons. You ever put a fist sized rock in a stocking and use it as a swinging club? Deadly, a dandy head buster."

They talked a few minutes. Some of the Circle S riders had been drifting out of town. The word was out that Gunnison had died and they were not as eager for the reward money on Spur's head now.

"I better check with Amy York. I don't imagine she ever stabbed anyone with a pair of scissors before."

When Spur knocked on the dressmaking shop door, he found it locked. He knocked again, then a third time. At last the shade over the door moved, a cautious eye looked out and then the door opened.

As soon as the door closed she was in his arms.

"Oh, glory! I'm so glad you're not killed. I didn't hurt your shoulder, did I? Did he shoot you? I hope I did what you wanted me to with the scissors."

Amy stopped suddenly. "Here I am running off at the mouth when I should be helping you to sit down and see how I can be a good nurse to you. Did you get shot again? I'm so sorry. Well, you're going to stay with me here tonight. I'll take care of you. That shoulder must hurt just terribly.

"I have a secret home remedy I make myself that will fix you up in no time. It's whiskey cut with some lemon juice." She grinned. "Might not be good medicine, but at least after three or four you won't feel much pain."

"Yes, thanks, I can use some of that medicine of yours."

She smiled and let out a long held breath. "Oh, good! I was afraid . . . I mean, you know I'm going to do my best to seduce you before the night is over."

Spur grinned. "Be right disappointed if you didn't, Amy. Be my pleasure, I can assure you."

She kept the shop closed, led Spur into the back to her apartment, and mixed a tall whiskey for him with lemon and a chunk of river ice.

"Most folks say you can eat our winter river ice. Some say it's tainted, but with enough whiskey to kill any bugs, I'm game if you are."

He pulled at the drink and felt the warmth hit his belly, then move outward. Spur sat on a big stuffed chair and relaxed. Things were moving better. The town was safer, the plan in motion to stop Cameron from selling off the stock. Time to take some time out and relax for a minute.

Amy came back in with some small sandwiches and another drink mixed for him. She had changed clothes and wore a softly clinging blouse. The way it outlined her large breasts, he was sure she wore nothing under it. She sat next to him on the arm of the big chair and leaned over and kissed his cheek. The blouse billowed open at the low neck and he could see all of one pink-tipped breast.

She moved back and smiled. "Spur McCoy, maybe we could give you the rest of your medicine later. Right now we should see if we remember how to make love."

Spur took a final drink from the glass and put it on a small table outside the chair. "Sounds like the best plan I've had all day." He held out his good arm. She kissed his lips, then took off the blouse and brought one of her breasts down to his mouth.

Spur McCoy moaned in delight and accepted the offering.

11

Spur McCoy relaxed on the soft bed. He lay propped up on two pillows and smoked a long black cigar as thin as his little finger. He deserved a short break from his rigorous schedule. The set pieces were in place to begin the harassment of Curt Cameron and his outlaw crew. Tomorrow or the next day the confrontation would begin.

Amy scurried into the room, all smiles and naked as was possible. Their first lovemaking had been fast and furious as she extracted her pound of flesh and raced him to a mutual climax.

The second time had been soft and lazy, with Amy on top pounding away like she was riding a fucking bucking bronco. When she had at last cooled down to a slow boil, she pulled away from him and kissed him.

"Time for the cook to get her big cock here some supper. Don't you go away!" She bent and kissed his softening penis.

"Christ, I haven't been fucked this good for five years," she laughed, "do you realize that! Frankly, I'd forgotten how good a man's prick jammed up my pussy feels. You can take it as gospel I sure as hell ain't waiting no damned five years again to get me a good fucking man."

She looked at him, her big breasts bouncing as she turned.

"You good for at least six times, right, on an all night fuck-out?"

Spur laughed, patted her breasts and then ran his hand down between her legs.

"At least six. What's for dinner?"

"Pussy!" she said and shrieked with laughter as she hurried out of the bedroom to the small kitchen. Rubens, the Flemish master portrait painter, would have loved Amy. She was all curves and solid heft with large breasts, a rounded tummy, a more than generous ass and thick arms and legs. Yes, Rubens would have loved painting Amy in the nude.

Spur pulled on his pants and went to the small kitchen. Amy was still naked, frying potatoes, onions and green peppers to go with the steak that was just turning medium rare in a heavy skillet on the wood burning kitchen range.

"Love to cook," Amy said. "Guess my size shows it, but I always say if a little is good, a lot of girl is better." She turned and watched him. "You got any complaints about the service in the bedroom so far?"

"None whatsoever," Spur said patting her fat fanny.

They ate quickly and hurried back to the bedroom.

"Something different," Amy said eyeing him as Spur slid out of his pants. His penis was flaccid now.

"You don't really like my fucking!" Amy screeched. "Look at your god damned shriveled up little worm of a prick! He's all soft. If you loved my screw you'd be hard again and ready to come in my face!"

He slapped her bottom and she bent over to give him a better target.

"Yes, spank me good. But I still say you don't like my kind of pussy if you go soft."

"A man can't stay hard all the time, or he'd pass out."

"Not so. My brother used to have a stiff dick for fourteen hours a day. He was fourteen years old at the time and I was a damned sexy sixteen. He'd show his stiff cock to me in the morning, and I'd see the bulge in his pants all day. We lived on a farm, and every chance he got when the folks weren't around, he'd flip his prick out and try to get into me.

"He got his first hard on when he was thirteen. He came into the outhouse when I had my skirt down and was bent over. He saw pussy for the first time that day and he screeched and grabbed his cock and instantly he was as hard as a pitchfork handle. He tried to jump me right there. I didn't let him, little prick.

"I made him wait until we got in the barn and I could really look at his dick. His balls were still almost hairless, but his dick hardened up to four-inches long. He played with my tits, which was as big when I was fifteen as they are now. I'd never had a hard prick to mess around with so I turned and pushed and pumped him a couple of times."

Amy laughed. "He touched my titties three times and he squirted cum all over my skirt. Then he wanted to play with my pussy too, but I said next time. Tell you the truth, I'd seen so many pregnant girls, I didn't want to get knocked up."

"What do you want to do different this time?" Spur asked.

"Something really strange, wild . . . sinful! She got on the bed on her hands and knees and looked at him.

"Like that?" Spur asked.

She took a deep breath and nodded.

"Which spot?"

"Oh, shit! Both of them!"

Spur moved behind her and spread some saliva

around her tight little bung and pushed.

"Jeeeeeeeeeeeeeeesus!" Amy howled as he slid past the restriction and lanced inside. "Oh, damn but that is low down and dirty! It's so strange, so fucking wild!" she fell down on her elbows on the bed, her big bottom still high and throbbing.

"You sure this is all right?" Spur asked.

"You stop now and I'll kill you!" she brayed as her voice went wierd and she climaxed so many times in a row that Spur lost track. He felt his own juices flowing and banged against her round bottom as hard as he could. Then she caved forward as he exploded inside and they lay there, both panting, sucking for breath.

Spur started to move.

"Stay put!" Amy shrilled. "I want him to go all soft right there. You take a little nap, you want to. I want this one to last as long as it will. Might not get a cock down my shit alley again for a long spell."

Spur laughed softly and took a nap on her soft buttocks and creamy back. She moved a short time later and he roused. He rolled away from her and she grinned.

"So fucking wonderful! So pussy fucking, cock fucking wonderful!" She looked over at him. "I never swear or talk dirty except in bed, have you noticed that? It just seems right. If we're fucking up an all night storm, might as well call a fuck a fuck and a pussy a pussy."

She got up and led him out to the kitchen and the wash basin. She poured out some water, took a wash cloth and sudsed his limp prick off well. Then she washed it again and rinsed him. By that time he was hard again.

"Christ, just like my brother. Once at Sunday dinner we had company and us kids had to sit close together. He was fourteen then and first thing he did was put his hand under the table where nobody could see it and reached over to my crotch. I left his hand there. It felt kind of good. When he tried to get me to spread my legs, I did.

"Damn that was wild, getting pussy-felt right there at the table with the whole family in sight and not knowing a damn thing 'bout it! Then he pulled on my arm and I put my hand down in my lap under the table and he brought it over to his crotch. He already had his stiff prick out of his pants. He cupped my fingers around it and pumped my hand up and down.

"By the time the main course came he groaned and pushed his finger right up my pussy. I was jacking him off like crazy and he shot his cum all over the underside of the living room table. I guess I yelped some too, because my father looked at me.

"'Amy, did you have something to say'?" he asked me. "I shook my head, sure my voice would be all crazy. Father nodded. " 'Good, because little girls should be seen and not heard.'

"We both sat up a little straighter then and ate our dinner. While we waited for dessert we played with each other again. I think that was the first time I really climaxed. Will had his two longest fingers stuck all the way up my cunny!"

Amy led Spur back to the big bed and they sat there all naked and flushed and warm and sexy and stared at each other.

"Spur, sweet prick, I want to suck you off. I want to take you all the way until you squirt your juice down my throat. Would you mind?"

Spur laughed softly and shook his head. "It's your night, Amy, whatever you want, wherever, and as many times as I can get it up."

She did. Spur couldn't remember the last time he'd been able to climax that way, but he sure did this time. Amy sucked and gulped and he fired his load.

It was nearly dawn when they at last stretched out on the bed and fell asleep. The only thing that woke them about nine the next morning was someone rattling the door.

"Oh, good gracious!" Amy said contritely. "I forgot I have a fitting for Mrs. Asamore this morning for that new dress. Spur McCoy, you dress your wonderful body and get it out the alley door. If Mrs. Asamore even suspects that I've had a man in my bed last night, she'd absolutely ruin my business. Now scoot!"

Spur got dressed and out the back door without being seen. He made his way to the hotel, found his shaving gear and scraped off two days of growth. Then he checked with the Shuntingtons and found them both up and edgy.

He told them about filing charges against Curt Cameron.

"Yes, about time we figured that out," Rutger said. "Might not work, but it should slow him down some."

"Spur McCoy, I need to talk to you," Priscilla said. "Am I free to do some shopping yet?"

"A few more days. Anyway, I like that dress. You look like a princess."

Spur left after a short visit to talk to the lawyer who said he would draw up the papers in the proper legal form right away.

He then went the long way to the back door of the jail and walked inside.

"Been looking for you, McCoy," Sheriff Dryer said. "Circle S has a thousand head of stock outside of town waiting to put them into the railroad stock yards. I talked to the buyer last night and he told the trail boss he would have to talk to me. He's due here in about half an hour. I'm certain that he won't come alone.''

They talked it over and Sheriff Dryer deputized six extra men, issued them shotguns and placed them as obvious guards around the front of the sheriff's office. Each double barreled whammer held three and a half inch double-ought buck rounds.

"The trail boss said he was sure Mr. Cameron himself would be here for the meeting,'' Sheriff Dryer said. "The man was fit to be roped and tied. Said he's never heard of no such thing as a brand check at a loading chute. I told him he hadn't been in my county very long, then."

Spur checked outside. The guards were in position, not hiding, in plain sight and positioned to give them a deadly cross fire and not endanger the other guards.

The Circle S men came right on schedule at 10:30. The man leading the ten riders could only be Curt Cameron. He was tall, broad shouldered and wore an expensive jacket over a gambler's vest and fancy frilly shirt hung with two gold chains and a diamond stick pin in his tie. The diamond was big enough to make every woman in town envious.

Cameron swung down from his mount, looped the lines around the hitching rail and waited for his nine men to do the same. All the riders were armed with pistols.

Spur walked outside the office with the Sheriff and waited. The ten moved between the shotgun guards, and some of the Circle S riders were starting to frown.

Sheriff Dryer held up his hand. "Cameron, that's far enough. The only thing we have to talk about is the herd you brought in to the edge of town. You can't ship them. There hasn't been a general roundup in the valley yet and there isn't a brand inspector in town. Soon as Harry gets back from Cheyenne, I'll have him check over your critters."

"Won't do, Sheriff," Cameron said, his voice strong, sure. "I've got approval of the cattle buyer to ship. If I don't get them on this train, I lose my cars."

"Talked with the buyer. He says he'll have more cars in a week or ten days. My advice is take this herd back to grass and fatten them up for ten days, then we'll be set up to check your brands and get them out of town."

"Won't do, Sheriff," Cameron said. "My close in range is near gone. I'd just run the fat off them if I went to a higher range and back. Won't do at all."

"Sorry, Cameron. As long as this is my county, we run it according to the law. No general roundup and brand checks, no shipment unless every head passes the brand inspector. You have some argument with that, contact your Wyoming Territorial legislator with a complaint."

Spur McCoy leaned against the front of the sheriff's office watching. Twice Cameron's glance took him in. Both times his eye twitched until he reached up and rubbed it with his hand. Now he turned to McCoy.

"This has to be your doing, McCoy. The ranch is mine, bought and paid for. The cattle are mine, the brands are mine. Nothing you can do will stop me from selling what I want to sell, and when I want to."

"Cameron, you aren't a captain of cavalry in the Confederate any more. Here we live by the law, not the power of a company of army riders. You'll do well to listen to what the sheriff has to say. He's the law here, you aren't."

Cameron started to say something, then stopped. He wheeled around, motioned to his men and they walked back to their horses.

"Oh, Cameron. I guess it's time I told you." The sheriff waited until the big man looked around.

"I'm enforcing a new law in Laramie. No gunfire allowed within the city limits. Anyone firing a weapon in town will be fined a hundred-dollars and put in jail for three months. You might let your men know about the new law. It's being enforced as of now. Noticed a lot of your men in town looking for a gun fight. You'd be doing them a favor to pull them out. They'll just get themselves in trouble or killed here in Laramie. Everyone be better off that way. Now, Mr. Cameron, you have a nice ride back to your ranch."

The shotgun guards had the weapons angled over their arms, pointing at the ground, ready to pull them up at a second's notice if needed. The ten riders from the Circle S watched the guards a moment. Curt swore at everyone he could see, but did so softly. Then he turned and walked back to the street and his horses.

Spur waited until the ten men were mounted and moved off to the north. Then he relaxed. When the men were almost out of town it sounded as if all ten emptied their revolvers into the air.

Spur grinned. "New law you have on the books, Sheriff?"

"Thinking about it, just thinking about it," he snorted. "The big talker had to swallow my slow-down. He figured on blowing me away with his army behind him. But he sure as hell changed his mind about that. You called him Captain. He really used to be in the war?"

"True. Somewhere, somehow. I haven't figured out exactly what he did, but we'll find out. Wonder what he'll do next?"

"He better drive that herd back to Circle S land or

he's going to have a visit from me and my new
deputies out there. My guess is that he'll take them
back. He'll work on some new plan, some better
idea."

"I'll probably hear about it. Right now I need to
check with that lawyer, then go see the kids."

Spur looked up and down the main street that
some were calling Third Street. He didn't see any of
the Circle S loafers he had spotted before. Most of
them had cleared out. But it only took one, and one
lucky shot.

He went through the alley to the hotel and up to
the third floor rooms. Priscilla let him in.

"Rutger said he wanted to talk to that lawyer you
mentioned. He's down there now. He promised me
that he would be extremely careful."

Spur closed the door and told her about how they
made Cameron back down at the sheriff's office.

"Then it really is true?" Priscilla asked. "Do we
have a chance of getting the ranch back?"

She wore a pretty dress that set off her com-
plexion, and now she perched primly on the edge of
the bed.

"More than a chance, a good chance," Spur said.

She stood and walked to him. She was just over
five-feet-four, and she smiled up at him proudly.

"I'm sure that between you and my brother you
can save the ranch. I . . . I just don't know what's
happened to mother and father. We'll find out
though."

She hesitated. For a moment he didn't think she
was going to go on. Then she seemed to plunge
ahead. "Mr. McCoy, you know about Mr. Parker . . .
what he did. I . . . I shouldn't be talking this way. It
was terrible, yet not all of it. I mean, he forced me,
and that was bad. But—"

She turned to the window and looked outside,

then went on without looking at Spur. "Well, after a while, when he had ripped my clothes off and there was nothing more I could do, then I rather . . . no, not that, but I wasn't terrified. After a while it seemed, I don't know, kind of natural I guess. What I'm wondering now. . . ."

She took a deep breath and turned to him, walked up and put her arms around his neck. Priscilla reached up on tip toes and kissed Spur on the lips.

"There. That wasn't so hard." She smiled. "Mr. McCoy, I really am curious now. I want to know what it feels like to have someone I know and respect make love to me. Would you help me?"

Spur took her arms from around his neck, walked her to the bed and sat her down. Then he stood in front of her.

"Priscilla, you're a beautiful young lady. Any man would be lucky to make love to you. But that's a job you should leave for your husband. Now, just hold on. You're young, you have years and years ahead of you.

"Right now we have to use every waking minute trying to figure out how to get the ranch back for the Shuntington family, and finding your father and mother."

"If I took off my blouse, would that persuade you?" she asked, unbuttoning the top two fasteners.

"No, Priscilla. My job is to get your ranch back, and I need to get working on that right now." He bent and kissed her cheek, then moved and kissed her lips. Her eyes were still closed when he straightened up.

"You stay right here in your room for the rest of the day, and tonight we'll all have supper together in the dining room."

Her eyes opened slowly and she nodded. Spur slipped out the door and heard her walk to it and turn the key in the lock.

Now he had to get ready for his next, and he hoped his last, trip to the Circle S ranch.

12

Spur went back to the lawyer's place. His name was Hascomb Bernard, a balding man in his sixties with a pince-nez, watery eyes and an egg sized goiter that hung like a bell on his throat below his right ear. Spur tried not to look at it.

Bernard and Rutger sat near his desk working over a pencilled draft. Both looked up as Spur came in.

"Afternoon," Spur said. "How is it going?"

"You know the judge won't be through for a month or more," Bernard said, a small frown growing.

"We know that," Rutger said. 'You just draft the papers and file them with the sheriff, or the district attorney, or whoever you have to, and make sure that a copy goes out to the Circle S ranch."

"That I can do. Hate to do all the work and not expect to go to trial."

"Do it," Spur said. "You'll get paid for your time."

Spur motioned Rutger to one side. "Looks like most of the Circle S men have left town. I think it's safe to have a civilized dinner tonight in the dining room at the hotel. About six. I'll meet you and Priscilla there."

Rutger nodded. "I'll be there. Now, what was that confrontation with Cameron all about and why wasn't I invited to the bloodletting?"

"Didn't want you to get killed. It came within a mare's whinny of being a shoot-out. We had more guns, six double-barreled shotguns with double-ought buck. I could almost hear Cameron figuring the odds. But we stopped him cold. He can't sell any cattle here in town, and he won't drive them to Cheyenne. He's not the type to work that hard."

"So he'll give up? That doesn't sound like a man who has done all this work and then walk away empty handed."

"Yeah, that's what bothers me. He gave up too easily today. Have to do some recon work tonight."

"Meaning you're riding to the ranch. I'm going with you."

"Might be good for you to get your feet wet in this thing. It isn't all fun and frolic out there. Somebody could get killed."

"I think Cameron has already killed my parents. I owe the bastard."

Spur took a long breath. If he were in Rutger's position, nothing could keep him away. "All right, Rutger. We'll go just before it gets dark. You still have that shotgun guard in front of Priscilla's door?"

Rutger said he did.

Spur and one of the Sheriff's special shotgun toting guards roamed the town for an hour after that but could find no Circle S brands on any of the horses at the hitching rails. They saw none of the loungers who Spur had suspected were Circle S riders looking for an extra bonus for Spur's head.

He got to the dining room at the Medicine Bow Hotel just as Priscilla and Rutger came in. Priscilla had slipped out and bought a new dress and she looked as pretty as a fresh bunch of spring flowers.

Her smile dazzled Spur as he took her arm and led her into the dining room.

"Prettiest girl in sixteen counties," Spur whispered in her ear, then kissed her cheek.

"It was all worth it!" Priscilla whispered back, her smile reserved just for him.

They all had steak, the house specialty, with family style bowls of vegetables, potatoes, a salad and tall glasses of brisk, iced tea. Spur ate his quickly, as was his fashion. Rutger ate about half of his pound-and-a-half sized steak, but Priscilla only nibbled on hers. Most of the time she spent watching Spur.

Once she reached out and touched his arm. "Spur, are you really going to ride out to the ranch tonight? Won't that be terribly dangerous? I mean, if we have Mr. Cameron and his men on the run now, shouldn't we just wait and see what they do? See what happens?"

"Priscilla, most things we do are dangerous. Right now it's important we know what's going on out there so we can get ready for it. If they get packed up and move on, we'll know about that too. Dangerous doesn't mean we're going to get hurt."

Her pretty, young face pouted for a moment. "If you do get hurt I'll never forgive myself. Please don't go."

"We need to go, Priscilla. We're not doing it just to keep busy. I'll be with Rutger so we'll protect each other. It's your job to smile as pretty as you can and send us out with your good wishes."

She smiled with an effort leaning toward him. She touched his hand and gripped it tightly.

"All right. But you be careful of your hurt shoulder. Now, you have my good wishes and a smile, but I'm going to need a reassuring hug before you go."

Spur nodded. "I think we can oblige you on that. I just don't want you to starve yourself to death."

"Oh, I'm not a big eater."

They left a few minutes later and Rutger insisted on paying for the meal. He caused a flurry when he gave the cashier one of the fifty-dollar bills. At last they found change.

Upstairs, Priscilla stood in front of Spur until he reached out and hugged her. She came to him openly, pushing her whole body against his in a needing embrace. He felt her breasts crushing against him and she sighed.

She looked up. "A goodbye kiss on the cheek for luck?" she asked.

He pecked her cheek and hugged her again with his good right arm and stepped back.

"Riding time," Rutger said. He wore a pair of old jeans, shirt and leather vest and his gun belt hung low on his right hip.

Full darkness ate up the tentative dusk by the time the pair of riders trotted onto Circle S land. Rutger stopped and stared around him.

"First time I've been on the home place since I left last fall," he said. "It feels good. This is my land, and I want it back!"

"Do what we can," Spur said.

They rode harder for fifteen minutes and stopped and listened for patrols. They sniffed the air for wood smoke from some lookout's campfire. They did not hear or smell anything. Twenty minutes later they came through open range from the north and down toward the Circle S ranch buildings.

Lights blazed in several windows. They had left their horses a quarter of a mile back tied to some brush near the Laramie river. Now they bellied up to a small rise less than fifty yards from the first corral. Spur's shoulder hurt like fire from the motion, but he settled down on the ground and the

pain eased. They could see a large camp fire blazing
up in the middle of the ranch yard.

Spur spotted more than a dozen men around the
fire. As they watched, thirty more men came from
the bunkhouse and the screen door on the ranch
house slammed.

Spur touched Rutger and they lifted up and
moved forward without making a sound. Spur
recognized Cameron as he came into the firelight.
He held up his hands and the men quieted their
chatter.

Rutger slid to the ground and Spur followed. They
were near the corral and beyond one of the barns.
Spur figured they could hear what was going on
from their vantage point.

"How about a little dance?" Cameron called to the
crowd of men that had grown to nearly fifty.

"Yeah, Captain!" someone yelled.

"Lucia, Lucia, Lucia!" the men chanted.

A woman stepped out of the darkness into the
light and the men pushed back from one side of the
fire to give her a stage. She danced to the picking of
a Spanish guitar and her movements were slow and
sensual. Then the tempo increased and the dance
became more erotic until at last she began a strip
tease, tearing off clothes and throwing them behind
her.

The men whistled and stamped and shouted, and
when the last binder came off her breasts, Lucia was
bare to the waist and the men screamed in delight.
She danced topless for several minutes, ending in a
simulated sexual encounter in the dust before the
men. Then she jumped up and vanished into the
darkness to a screaming, cheering response.

Cameron stood up in the light and waited for the
cheering to stop. When it tailed off he waved his
hands.

"Now to business. We've got a complication. The

sheriff has gone sour on us. He suddenly is
demanding a brand inspection because there hasn't
been a general roundup and brand sorting. Says his
inspector is out of town for ten days."

"Bastard must be wise to us," somebody called.

"Damn close. Or McCoy is prodding him. We
could wait the ten days and protect our investment
here. But my feeling is that then there would be
some new problem. We're not going to score the way
we hoped here."

A wave of chatter rumbled over the crowd.

"But we still have a damned good chance to make
some big money. Way I figured it, we slip out of our
legal operation this time. There's a dandy little bank
in town that usually has a good sized amount of
cash on hand in the vault. We take the vault, we
strip every cash register in town, and then we crack
open the safe on the Union Pacific express car when
it rolls into Laramie."

"Yeah! Just like old times, Captain!" one of the
men shouted.

There were three cheers for the captain. The men
stood and shrieked their pleasure. A dozen rebel
yells pierced the dark night air.

"Now we're really going to live again!" one voice
boomed.

Cameron got them calmed down. "It ain't gonna
be no walkover," he called over the voices. "We've
got to plan it out and do it right."

"Damn, we're gonna ride hard again!" a voice
shrilled.

Everyone cheered.

Cameron grinned and calmed them down. "Don't
know for sure just how soon we'll go. You'll know in
time to pack your saddle bags. That's all you're
supposed to own, right?"

"Hey, damn it to hell, Captain. We gonna be able
to get us some women this time?"

Cameron scowled. "That gets tricky. Sometimes a man will chase you to hell and back if you poke into his pretty. We might have to hold off this time."

"Christ, Captain, we been holding off for three years." Half the men jeered the response and Cameron listened.

He threw up his hands. "Hell, why not? We'll bust this little town wide open and take anything and everything and any pretty woman we want!"

· The men cheered for five minutes and Cameron at last waved at them, rolled out a keg of beer, and walked back toward the ranch house.

Spur looked over at Rutger. Even in the darkness he could see the grim lines on the young man's face.

"At least they're moving on," Rutger said.

"But they could burn down Laramie and all your ranch buildings before they go."

"We can't let them do that," Rutger said, his voice tight. "They could also kill a lot of people, rape a lot of our women."

"We won't let that happen. We'll be ready for them in town. About the ranch—"

"Yeah, I know. Nothing we can do about it if they decide to torch it before they leave. What else can we do here?"

"I want to check the smaller barn back there."

"You're looking for graves, aren't you, Spur?"

"Yes. Two graves, or thirty-five, I don't know how many. You must have known some of the hands on your ranch. Would they just have packed up and left without talking to anyone in town?"

"Not unless there was a mighty potent threat hanging over their heads . . . like getting their guts blown out by a shotgun."

"Way I figure, too. Let's check that barn."

They eased away from the ranch yard, circled around a corral, but saw no guards. At the smaller barn they found no livestock, only hay and some feed grain stored in sacks and some in bins. Spur used a pitchfork and probed the floor under the hay and in the open areas, but could find no soft spots where there could be a grave. It was awkward work with his wounded left arm, but he made it.

Rutger stood by the door watching the bonfire. "Sure wish to hell you had some more of that dynamite you used to stampede that herd. I'd throw about a dozen sticks around that fire."

"Not sure we want them to know we're here," Spur said. "We want to surprise them when they ride in to take the town."

"How about their horses?" Rutger asked. "We could open the gate and they'd never know how it happened!"

Spur chuckled. "Why not?"

They moved cautiously to the main corral where about forty head of horses milled around. The gate was a swing type with a wire loop holding the top and the bottom pole in another wire loop. Spur lifted the top loop off, pulled the gate pole out of the lower loop and dragged the gate open six feet.

He went around one side of the corral and Rutger moved the other way, gently urging the horses toward the opening. The nags wandered out. A stampede would have alerted the outlaws. It took them five minutes but by then all but one horse was out the gate heading for the open range at a walk.

Spur and Rutger moved along after them, then cut to the north where they had left their horses.

The pair had mounted and ridden around the ranch and were well south before they heard the shouts of alarm from the men around the bonfire. Somebody must have checked the corral or found a wandering horse.

Spur and Rutger rode faster for a while until they were well away from the ranch.

"What did the men mean, just like old times?"

Rutger asked Spur as they rode through the softly cool darkness toward town.

"Not sure. These men don't impress me as being soldiers, but they were. You ever heard of Quantrill?"

"Sure. He was a Confederate officer who led a gang of murderers, robbers and rapists along the border during the war. He was supposed to raid the north and send the money and loot to the southern treasury. Most folks think he kept most of it for himself."

"Right you are. In 1863 he raided Lawrence, Kansas with four-hundred fifty men. They burned and pillaged the whole town and killed over one-hundred and fifty men, women and children. He turned into a scavengering outlaw after the war until he was hunted down by a federal force in Sixty-Five. He was wounded and died a month later. Cameron could have had the same kind of outfit near the end of the war. That would explain all the military jargon."

"You mean he's held a group like that together for six or seven years?"

"Could be. At least we have a better idea now what we're up against, a military force that's going to attack Laramie in the next day or so. We have to get to the sheriff and organize some form of defense, put out some outposts, the whole damn thing!"

"Lots of the men in town were in the war," Rutger said. "At least they know how to shoot a gun."

"Good. What we need is to get organized. We'll ride straight to the sheriff and see what he has to say."

"You were in the war, weren't you, Spur? You'd be the man I'd pick to put the whole thing together. I mean, you know what we need to do."

"We'll see," Spur said.

An hour later they sat in the sheriff's office. He

glowered at them and puffed on his pipe. The room was a blue pall of tobacco smoke.

"You're telling me we're going to have a damn Confederate army unit come boiling into town shooting us up?"

"Exactly what I mean, Sheriff. We finally put it all together. My suspicions are that Cameron operated a raider unit near the end of the war, something like Quantrill. After the war he kept them together and they operated as an outlaw band. Whatever, there's gonna be about fifty soldiers heavily armed come storming into Laramie in the next couple of days."

"Damn, we'll meet army with army. We got Ft. Sanders a mile outside of town. They should be able to throw up a hundred mounted troopers to meet any such attack."

Spur shook his head. "Wish they could, Sheriff. Remember that law Congress passed a few years ago. It prevents the military from taking part in any civilian law or policing operation. The congress was afraid we were heading toward martial law."

"The hell, you say? You mean if the Indians were attacking us, the army could help. But if it's just a bunch of white rabble they can't lift a saber?"

"Afraid so. But there may be one glimmer of hope. I can show the army my credentials and then if I can prove to the Fort commander that this is a unit of the Confederate army, I just might have a chance. I'll ride out there first thing in the morning. In the meantime, we better get our own troops together. How many deputies you got, including those six from today?"

"Nine."

"That's a start. How many able bodied men in town who own rifles?"

"Hell, maybe fifty or sixty. We had a sight more

before the Union Pacific moved so many of its people down the line.''

"How do we get them organized?''

"Not me. You're the expert, McCoy. I'll turn the whole damn thing over to you. I never was in the army.''

Spur nodded. "Fine. Here's what I want you to do. Tomorrow morning send your deputies into every store and to every house in town. Tell them what's happening, and ask the men to volunteer with their rifles and pistols. Probably won't happen tomorrow, but we need to be ready by noon.

"Have all the men report to your office here and I'll have a defense plan set up and position everyone. We'll put out three men as lookouts to spot the Cameron raiders before they get here. In the meantime, I'll be heading for the fort and try to make my case. If it doesn't work, we still have a way to defend ourselves.''

"Sounds good. What about the women and children?'' the sheriff asked.

"We'll keep them barricaded in their homes. Better than grouping them all at one spot.''

Spur paced the floor a minute, then grabbed his hat. "Right now I want to look over the town. They probably will come from the north, all in one bunch, since they won't know that we found out they're coming.'' He waved and went out the door with Rutger close behind.

They walked to the hotel, got a big tablet and three pencils from the room clerk, then made a rough map of the town starting at the northern trail outskirts.

Spur's arm still bothered him. He could move it, and he had his shirt on, but still the shoulder was stiff and it hurt to lift his arm. He was in no shape for a fistfight.

Back at the hotel in Spur's room, they checked the sketches and Spur began to make a plan. He would need at least three scouts out two miles from town. They would be his forward observers and would race for town the moment they saw the Cameron Raiders coming. Then the placement of the men.

He hesitated. It was late. He would think better in the morning. Maybe the army would help them do the job. Maybe. Spur said good night to Rutger and lay on his bed thinking about it. He had to use the best arguments he could at Fort Sanders, and his rank of full colonel. Even that might not be enough.

It took Spur two hours to get to sleep.

13

Spur found the leaflet under his hotel room door when he woke up. The page sized warning had this headline:

RAIDERS TO HIT LARAMIE!

Below it told concisely what the sheriff expected to happen to Laramie in the next twenty-four hours and asked all able bodied men to report with their weapons at the sheriff's office at noon.

The sheriff had been busy last night. Spur dressed, had a quick breakfast and rode out of the livery stable on his roan heading south. He hadn't been to the fort, mainly because he did not expect to need any help. But now he had a handle on the outlaws, and he was sure that the town needed the army's help.

When he rode into the familiar looking fort with the buildings and large parade grounds in the center, Spur almost felt like he was back in the army. It had been a tremendously important and terrifying and maturing part of his life.

He gave his horse to an orderly who directed him to the fort commander's office. The smell of the room when he opened the door gushed back memories: leather and paper, lots of raw wood and more leather and the smell of polish and gun oil.

A sergeant with a full beard met him. "Yes sir, what can we do for you, sir?"

Spur handed the sergeant the usually concealed identification form that certified that Spur McCoy was a full colonel in the United States Army on special assignment and should be accorded all proper respect.

The sergeant saluted at once. Spur returned the salute.

"I'd like to see the Fort Commander," Spur said.

"Yes sir. Let me tell him you're here." The sergeant took the identification form with him and hurried through a door into the adjacent office.

He returned almost at once.

"Major Patrick O'Reilly will see you, sir. Right this way."

Again the memories: a big U.S. flag on the wall, a picture of President Ulysses S. Grant behind his desk, two chairs and a bench, two rifles on the wall, a spittoon at the side of the battle scarred work place.

At the corner of the desk stood a man ramrod straight in his carefully tailored blue army uniform. He saluted smartly and Spur returned the formal greeting. Major O'Reilly was stubby, square, solid, and looked like the ideal mold of a perfect cavalry-man. His face was sunburned but a white line around his forehead showed where his campaign hat usually protected his head from wind, sun, rain and weather. Piercing gray eyes stared at Spur a moment. He had a moustache but no beard.

"Colonel McCoy, good to meet you. Have a seat. We have few visitors out this way."

"Major, I have an urgent problem and I need your help. I'm in Laramie on a delicate mission and now I find the remnants of a Confederate force of some fifty men. I suspect they were Quantrill type raiders near the end of the war. They've taken over the Circle S, the biggest ranch in the Bull Pen Valley, and now they are threatening to sack Laramie the way Quantrill did to Lawrence, Kansas back in Sixty-Three, I think it was."

"Confederate raiders? That's hard to believe, Colonel. It's been six years since the war was over."

"True, but this man, Curt Cameron, seems to have turned the trick."

"They wear uniforms?"

"No."

"Then what leads you to believe they are men of the Gray?"

"I've questioned one when he lay near death. Death bed confessions are seldom lies."

Major O'Rielly stood and walked around. He offered Spur a cigar, then lit one himself. He walked and puffed. After half a dozen circles of the office he stopped and tapped off the ash in the spittoon, hitting it dead center.

"Sir, if you say they are Confederate renegades, I'll have to accept your evaluation. However, that doesn't give me the right, under the new law Congress passed, to engage inforce of arms against them."

Spur started to say something but the Major held up his hand.

"Sir, if you would permit me to finish. The Congress was specific in its regulations. The army may engage in battle with nations and peoples the United States is in a state of war with. We no longer are in that state against the former Confederacy or its soldiers. Therefore, my troopers can't help you."

Spur blew smoke in the major's direction.

"But if the Cheyenne were preparing the same kind of a raid against Laramie, the army would ride to its defense?"

"Absolutely. The army is in a state of war against all hostile Indians within the boundaries of the United States and its territories."

"But, damnit, O'Reilly. I know these are rebs. I've heard their rebel calls. I heard them say it would be just 'like old times during the war' to raid and rape. . . ."

"I understand your dilemma, Colonel, indeed I do. But you can understand mine. There is no absolute evidence that these are rebel renegades. If there was I would bend the law a little and engage. But on the evidence you've given me, I'd be court martialed within two weeks."

Spur looked out the window at a company of cavalry drilling on the parade ground.

"Major, I was afraid that you might be a book soldier. We are now in the process of gathering up every rifle and pistol in Laramie and preparing for the assault. We'll do the best we can with the manpower and guns available. The matter is closed.

"Now, on to a more interesting subject. My orders instruct you to cooperate in every legal and proper way possible. I believe that's the wording."

"Yes, sir. As long as it's legal, I'll be glad to cooperate."

Spur smiled. "Good, Major. I'd like to have a review and inspection of two companies of your troops. I want to see a field bivouac with tents a quarter mile north of Laramie. Your people are to set up their camp there at one P.M. today and remain in place until tomorrow evening, at which time I will inspect the troops." He looked over at the major who was smiling.

"During this period of time, Major, your men should be engaging in drills including rifle target practice aimed to the north. Have I made my request and my instructions clear to you, Major O'Reilly?"

"Absolutely clear, sir. I see no problem with your request. We'll be glad to put on a show of strength. However, you must understand—"

"I know, Major. If the bluff does not work, you will not be expected to engage in any action against the rebels."

Spur looked out the window.

"Major, there is one section of army regulations I'm sure you are familiar with."

Major O'Reilly looked up quickly, a questioning expression on his face.

"If any unit of the United States Army is attacked or fired upon by any force, that unit is permitted to return fire and to defend itself at the discretion of the unit commander and to engage in direct action against such a force."

"Goddamn! You're right! Be more than glad to wait for the first shot from those damned rebel renegades!"

"If you have any problem in channels with your report, I'll be glad to send along a letter. If that doesn't help, the President will be more than happy to add his congratulations to your efforts which should negate any general problems you may have."

Major O'Reilly held out his hand. "You're a damned good man to have in his corner. We'll see you in Laramie about noon time."

Spur returned a friendly salute and hurried out to his horse. It had been rubbed down and curried and was ready for him at the door. Word travels fast when a visiting full colonel is on any army post.

Back in Laramie, Spur talked to the sheriff.

"Telegraphed Cheyenne to send the territorial militia. Turns out Wyoming doesn't have any, not yet. Also told the Union Pacific to stop its train outside of town if they heard any shooting in here."

Spur filled in the sheriff about what the army would do.

"That might solve our problem. Curt might see all those blue uniforms and turn tail."

"Might, but I've seen lots of men killed on a might. We keep doing all we can to get ready for a fight. How many men we have signed up?"

"Don't know until noon."

Spur went out and with his sketch of the town, picked out the places he wanted his best shots. Some on rooftops, some behind corners of buildings, some in wagon boxes.

At one o'clock they had forty-five men with rifles and pistols milling around outside the sheriff's office. Spur divided the men into those with military experience and those without. He took the ex-soldiers and spotted them at his selected spots. Then he filled in the north part of town with the rest of the twenty men who could shoot but hadn't been soldiers. Most of these men had never even shot at another human being, let alone killed one.

When the men were in place he told them to memorize their position. They would ring the school bell when the lookouts spotted the rebels coming.

Spur had kept three men for the lookouts. All appeared to be tough and self assured. He led them a mile north out of town, found no suitable spots and moved another mile. There he placed one at the river, another one each side about a half mile apart.

He told each the same thing. "If you see a troop coming, make damn sure it's forty or fifty men, then ride like hell for town. Fire your pistol twice as a signal. I want all three of you into town and then you mix with the other defenders."

Spur left the lookouts in place, telling them he would replace them at dusk or have them come in. He didn't expect a night attack by the raiders.

Back in town, Spur released the men from their defensive positions and put everyone to work boarding up store windows. Some of the merchants had already started. Windows were not big on most of the stores, but glass had to be brought in all the way from Chicago or St. Louis and it was expensive.

By two o'clock all was ready. Spur rode out of town to the north and saw about eighty cavalrymen setting up a bivouac. Major O'Reilly was with the men and he saw that the small tents were set up so they crossed the main trail to the north.

Spur rode up and took the salute.

"Progressing nicely, Colonel." O'Reilly said. "Camp will be set up in another five minutes. Then we will engage in drills and hold our target practice until your scouts return with word of hostiles. Each of my men has a hundred and twenty rounds.

"Oh, I took the liberty of sending out three scouts to watch and observe and learn from your men."

Both old soldiers laughed.

"Thanks. Not even sure Curt Cameron will come when he sees all of this spit and polish and blue uniforms. Hope to hell they don't. Then again, I hope they do. That murdering mob can't just be turned lose to ply their dirty trade somewhere else."

"Exactly why we're here, Colonel McCoy. About time their renegade raiding days were cut short, damn short, and deep, at least six-feet underground."

Spur nodded, turned and rode back into town.

Sheriff Dryer had been grinning ear to ear when he saw the army setting up tents.

"Curt will never have the nerve to come into town past that many U.S. Army regulars," Dryer said.

"Let's hope. Oh damn! What about ammo? I want every man to have at least fifty rounds of ammunition." Spur ran out to the street and began to spread the word. Fifty rounds. Men scattered to get more rounds from home, and from stores. The

hardware man and the general store man brought
out their entire stock and doled it out to whoever
needed it.

"No charge, damn right no charge!" the hardware
man said. "What good are cartridges going to do me
if them Rebs put a couple of rounds through my
skill? Help yourself." He hesitated. "Course, after
this is all over, if you got any rounds left over, I'd
appreciate having them back."

Spur checked with the sheriff. Both men were on
their horses to get around town faster. "When is the
train due?"

"We usually have a four-thirty. Curt knows that.
He might time his hit to catch the train here."

"I would if I was in his boots," Spur said. As the
minutes slipped by, more and more of the men
moved back to their assigned guard positions
without being told.

Spur tipped a cold glass of lemonade the hotel
handed out. He made one more ride around the town
to check the men. Out north of the Markham house
he could see the blue troopers doing company
horsemanship drills. Damn, they looked good! Just
seeing all those blue shirts and pants and soft brown
campaign hats gave Spur more confidence than he
had been able to work up before.

He knew what a trained company of raiders could
do. They would shoot up the town, burn it down,
rape the women, kill every man they could find. It
could be devastation!

But with the Pony Soldier troopers . . . would
they be fired at by Curt's men? All it would take was
one hot headed rebel. Pray for that one to lose his
nerve and shoot. Just one!

At three-fifteen, Spur rode to the north end of
town where Third Avenue emptied into the trail
north. He could see his men on rooftops and behind
fences and in wagons. If Curt and his men came

through the troopers and into town, and if they stayed bunched as they charged forward. . . .

Damnit! Too many IF's!

Far off Spur thought he heard the sound of two shots.

The signal? Were they coming? Was it his imagination?

He stood in the saddle and looked where he had left the first man. A thin trail of dust rose into the air. A man was coming! Then two more thin trails, and two more pistol shots.

"They're coming!" Spur bellowed. "The scouts are coming in which means the rebels must be heading our way. Every man get ready. Fifty rounds. Don't fire at the rebels until you hear my command. Does everyone understand?"

He saw heads nod. Saw men's nervous faces. A few responded with a yea, then all vanished back into their hiding places.

Spur rode north to the troopers. They had heard the shots, their own scouts were riding hell-bent-for-breakfast toward the troop.

Major O'Reilly cantered up and saluted.

"I'd say your renegades are on the way. We'll do our duty here. We either help you or we don't. It's up to the rebels."

"Understood. Good luck!"

Spur galloped forward and met the first scout.

"Coming, Mr. McCoy! Must be at least fifty of them. They all got rifles and pistols and they're riding hard!"

"Fine. We're ready. Get up on the roof, over there. Don't shoot until I give the order. Go!"

He talked to the other two lookouts who gave him the same story.

Spur moved his horse behind a house, climbed the ladder nailed to the rear and stepped out on the second floor porch roof. He carried his Spencer rifle

with. him and now lay down and peered over the
wooden parapet.

He could see the cloud of dust from the two
hundred hooves as they charged toward town. Out
maybe two miles.

The army had drawn up in a double company
front, with eighty men on horseback side by side
looking north and stretched across the trail for forty
yards on each side. It made a formidable sight and
Spur was sure it would have an effect on the rebels.

He watched them come. Spur turned to the town
from his high point.

"They are coming!" he bellowed. "Women and
children inside. Rifles on the roofs and pistols in the
open windows. Make every shot count. Nobody fires
until I give the signal. We'll suck them in as far as
possible, then let go."

He watched the dust. A mile out. Then a half mile.
The front riders could see the blue line of troopers
drawn up across the trail now no more than four-
hundred yards from the rebels.

Spur bellied down on the roof. He hadn't even felt
his hurt shoulder as he climbed the ladder putting
his weight on the arm. Now it throbbed, but he knew
once the action started the hurt would be forgotten.
He held the rifle muzzle at the very edge of the
gingerbread on the roof line and waited.

Curt Cameron scowled as what he thought he saw
turned out to be the real thing. Eighty, maybe a
hundred blue shirted Yankee soldiers had camped
outside Laramie and now were stretched in a
company front across the trail blocking it!

What the hell, the war was over. The Bluebellies
couldn't mess in civilian police work. Congress had
passed the law. He knew all about that law.

So what were the troopers doing?

He held up his hand and slowed the gallop.

A trap. It could be some kind of a trap.

"No firing until my command!" Curt barked and heard the orders repeated to the rear of the herd of horsemen. He thought about it again. Yeah, a trap.

"No man fires at the Yankee Bluebellies or he gets his head blown off by me!" Curt bellowed. Again the words were passed back until every man heard.

Curt slowed the riders again, then at last when they were within fifty yards, he walked the men forward. Twenty yards from the line he halted the riders and moved out five steps.

"Who is in command here?" he yelled.

Major O'Reilly kicked his sorrel forward three steps and stopped.

"Major O'Reilly, sir, and are you Captain Cameron?"

"Curt Cameron, the war is over. Give way for my party to pass. You're blocking a public roadway."

"Not so, Captain. We're in a mock battle defending this roadway in an entirely legal war exercise against a simulated attack by a force of five-hundred Cheyenne. I'll have to ask you to go around if you want to proceed."

Curt felt his temper flaring. He held it in check, tried to calm himself. He whipped his horse around, and in spite of himself gave a cavalry hand signal to his men to turn and follow him.

Damn! He had been tricked. They knew, somehow they knew. He'd give a hundred dollars to gun down that Bluebelly Major!

The men behind him grumbled.

"Stand steady!" he bellowed as they rode to the left. Curt had turned the lead men around the last Yankee and headed for the north end of town when he sensed trouble. The men at the end of his ragged cluster of men were grumbling. He picked up the pace and soon the last of his men had cleared the last Yankee. Then he swore as he heard a single pistol shot.

The last Yankee in the line crumpled and fell off his horse.

"Return hostile fire!" Major O'Reilly bellowed.

Curt's force galloped toward the town. The Pony Soldiers swung their horses around in a moment of confusion, then the line steadied and eighty rifles lifted and the roar of shots deafened the men for a moment. A third of the troopers had Spencer repeaters and the guns spoke again and again.

Spur McCoy hardly believed it. In the three-hundred yards to the north end of town from the soldiers, he saw half the Cameron Raiders shot off their horses. Not more than twenty-five lived to reach the safety of the town.

The army rifles ceased fire as the Raiders came close enough to town to put the defenders there in the line of fire.

Spur let Curt Cameron and his survivors gallop into the "safety" tunnel between the first two houses before he bellowed.

"FIRE AT WILL!"

A dozen rifles spoke at once. Six men slammed off their horses, dead before they hit the ground. Now there was a steady snapping of rifle shots as the riders came in sight of one layer of gunmen after another defending their town.

Only seven of the Raiders remained on their horses as they charged through the narrow street to the first alley. They whipped down it and out of range and rode out of town as fast as their lathered mounts would take them.

"CEASE FIRE!" Spur shouted into the sudden silence.

The whole fire fight in town had lasted only twenty seconds. Slowly the men on the ground came out and kicked rifles and pistols away from the

Cameron Raiders on the ground whether they were dead or wounded.

Spur caught his horse and rode out of town toward the army camp. Troopers were checking the dead, moving the wounded into a staging area, and taking care of the small war as it should be done.

Major O'Reilly cantered up on his horse.

"We have one trooper wounded, Colonel. The rest of my men are untouched. So far we have an enemy casualty count of twenty-two dead and six wounded."

"Six or seven of them got away down the alley," Spur said. "Curt Cameron is one of the dead. He'll never lead another pillaging raid on anyone."

"Except maybe in hell," Major O'Reilly said. He nodded. "I'd say it was a good exercise. You want the wounded? We'll trade you our six wounded for the dead raiders. I'd say a large common grave out here somewhere would serve the purpose as well as any. Were any of your people casualties?"

Spur laughed, the tension broken. "I forgot to check. It's been some time since I've been in a battle." He turned and rode back into town. He suddenly felt so limp he thought he might fall off the saddle.

Aftershock. He'd seen it a hundred times in a battle, and after a battle.

In the street the Laramie defenders gathered around the wounded and the dead.

"Any of our people wounded?" Spur called.

Rutger came from the crowd.

"No sir, not a one. I checked."

"Good. Rutger, get a wagon and some help and load on the dead. The Army is going to dig the graves. One large one, the major said. Then tell Doc Asamore he's going to have about ten new patients.

Already some of the men were pulling nails out of

the boards that had been put over the store
windows. Curtains were going up. Spur turned and
rode back to the north. He would gladly take the
wounded and get them patched up and sent on their
way, but not before he grilled each one about what
happened at the Shuntington ranch when Curt took
it over.

That was his next job.

14

Five of the wounded from the Battle of Laramie could walk. Spur found them heavily guarded by the Sheriff's deputies at Doc Asamore's office. Spur took them on one by one.

The first two just stared at him and wouldn't say a word. He backhanded each across the face and went on to the next one on the bench. He was younger, had been crying. His left shoulder had been shattered by a round and another sliced through his thigh. He had lost a lot of blood but was not in serious condition.

"Name?" Spur barked at him.

"Billy Joe Hatcher."

"Where were you born, Billy Joe?"

"Memphis, Tennessee."

"You were in the Confederate army then. What was your rank?"

"Private, the Tennessee Fourth."

"Shut up, you asshole!" one of the other rebels shouted.

Spur ignored the soldier.

"You been with Captain Cameron since the war?"

"Yes sir."

"He's dead, you know."

The young man sniffed, tears flowed from his eyes

169

as he nodded.

"We know that your band has taken over ranches before, the way you did the Circle S. Can you tell me about it?"

"You do, Billy Joe and you're one dead reb," the same voice from down the bench said.

Spur spotted the man this time. He jumped in front of him, slammed a right fist into his face, smashing him back against the wall. He hung there a minute, eyes wide, then he passed out.

Spur took Billy Joe outside and sat him on a bench behind the doctor's office.

"Not sure what's in store for you, Billy Joe, but I know the sheriff is going to charge every one of you. If you tell me exactly what happened when you and Curt rode into the ranch, I'll see that you get off, and that as soon as you're able, you can jump on board the train free and clear with no charges against you and head back to Tennessee."

Billy Joe stifled his sobs and looked up. "No lie? You'd help me get clear?"

"Word of honor, Billy Joe. I'm with the United States Secret Service. I never go back on my word. Were you along with the first of the raiders when they hit the ranch?"

Billy Joe nodded.

"Tell me about it, Billy Joe. Exactly what happened."

Billy Joe wiped his eyes with his sleeve. The doctor's wife came out the back door.

"This one special?"

"Yes. He's helping me. Can you patch him up out here away from the others?"

"Of course. We're just all so thankful you helped save our town. Laramie will remember you for a long, long time, Mr. McCoy."

Spur thanked her and looked back at Billy Joe. "Tell me what happened when you first rode in to the Shuntington ranch. Was it night time?"

"Yeah. Night. After midnight. Curt said it would be easiest that way. Catch them all sleeping. No guards out, he'd checked. He'd been in town for a week making arrangements.

"He met us about a mile from the ranch and led us in, all fifty-eight of us. We had over two-hundred at one time right before the war ended. We did good then, raiding Yankee outposts and some farms and a village here and there.

"But now we was down to fifty-five. We rode in and some of the men were assigned to the bunk-house. First they went around the bunks and picked up all the six-guns and rifles they could find. Then they woke up the cowboys and ordered them all to get dressed.

"They didn't know what was happening. One big guy refused to put his pants on so one of our guys shot him in the shoulder. After that they all did exactly what they were told.

"Curt said only thing to do with the hands was to kill them all or make them think we was going to kill them so they would never come back. We got them outside and brought around their horses. Then we roped them all together and ten of our men herded them off the ranch and rode them for five days west. By the time they had them that far most were so sick and hungry they could hardly ride. The guys pushed them into a little town to recover and warned them that if any of them showed up in Laramie or if they talked about what happened, somebody would know and would shoot them until they looked like a kitchen colander. They was scared damn good."

"Then what happened back at the ranch?" Spur asked.

"I went up to the ranch house just after we arrived. I'm good with the women folk. Curt always had me handle them until he figured out what to do. We went into the house, found the bedroom and picked up the two pistols close by the bed. Then Curt woke up the couple in the bed.

"They was surprised, mad as hell, and the man, Shuntington kept swearing and trying to fight. One of our guys, Bryce, kept knocking him down. Finally he couldn't get up any more.

"Curt took this Shuntington out to the kitchen table and tried to get him to sign the bill of sale and the grant deed, but he wouldn't. Brought out his woman and ripped her nightgown off and squeezed her tits but even when she screamed her husband wouldn't sign.

"Curt put the woman up on the table on her back and said he was going to fuck her right in front of him. That's when the guy went crazy. He grabbed a frying pan and brained Bryce with it, split open his head like a watermelon, and then he came at Curt.

"Curt had plenty of notice and he had out his Colt. He shot the guy five times and had to jump out of the way as Shuntington fell dead at his feet.

"The old woman screamed and wailed, but Curt went ahead and screwed her there on the table. Didn't even take his pants down, just opened his fly. She screamed at the top of her voice the whole damn time. Then he shot her right in her open mouth and her brains flew all over the kitchen. Then Curt laughed and shot her through each eye.

"Billy Joe," he told me. "Drag these bodies out of here and get somebody to bury them. Dig them in deep where nobody will find them."

Billy Joe looked up at Spur, his eyes pleading.

"I come right off the farm into the army. They sent me to Captain Cameron and he trained us well. We wasn't usual infantry, we went back and forth across the lines. Always had on civilian clothes. He called us his raiders.

"I never killed nobody 'cept in a straight shoot-out. Never did murder nobody like Curt and the others did."

"I understand, Billy Joe. Where did you bury the Shuntingtons?"

"In the garden. The lady had a big garden in back of the ranch house and she watered it from the river, a canal she had dug to bring water to it year round. Grew some good vegetables back there and had a peach tree and things. Half of it was all ploughed up ready for more planting.

"I had the guys dig it deep, down at least six feet. Then we covered it over and transplanted some vegetables over the spot. Both of them are in one hole. We wrapped them up in blankets first. Figured it was the Christian thing to do. I even said some words softlike as we filled in the hole."

Spur watched the young man. He wasn't over twenty-two or three. Must have been sixteen when he joined the group. What an education in butchery he must have had!

"After we get you fixed up, I'll want you to show us where the bodies are," Spur said.

"Yes sir, I sure will do that."

Spur kicked the bench, hard. Then he took Billy Joe back to the doctor who examined his wounds. Nothing was broken. He bandaged the leg and shoulder and gave Billy Joe back to Spur.

The sheriff himself rode out to the ranch with them. Billy Joe sat the horse carefully, his arm and leg hurting. Spur had little sympathy for him.

"What kind of charges on the raiders?" Spur asked.

"Talked to the district attorney. We've got attempted murder, discharging a firearm at a person, rioting, conspiracy to rob and plunder, half a dozen more. Probably drop all but the attempted murder charge and put them away in the territorial prison for ten to fifteen years."

"All except Billy Joe here?" Spur said.

"Who? Oh, the one who got away. Nothing pending on him at all. Sooner he gets on the train headed east the better. Tomorrow morning would be a good time."

Spur had brought along two men he hired in a saloon to do the digging. In the end he helped. They lifted the blanket-wrapped bodies out of the grave. All of them around the grave had kerchiefs over their noses but it didn't help much. A month old corpse is a highly decomposed piece of flesh.

The blanket-covered bodies were put in the barn and one of the men left as a guard.

Spur heard the noise again and stared at the house. They hadn't been inside.

"Somebody's in the house," Spur said. He ran for it with his six-gun out. The back door was half open. He toed it all the way out and slid inside.

A woman stood by the kitchen table watching him.

"Why you dig them up?" she asked.

"Who are you?"

"Lucia."

"Oh, yes, the topless dancer. You were the one dancing in the firelight last night. You were good."

"Thanks. Where are the men?"

"Curt is dead, along with about thirty of his outlaws. You were with them?"

"Not with them, I'm heading for St. Louis in the morning. I just met them two months ago."

"Why St. Louis?" Spur asked.

"I have some business there."

"Fair enough. You want to ride with us back to town?"

"Might. It's getting lonely here."

Spur nodded. "Get your things, we'll be leaving in half an hour."

Spur found a horse in the corral and saddled it for her. He didn't care if she wore a split skirt or not, she was riding the horse with a regular saddle.

When he came back to the house she was ready. She wore a pair of man's pants she had cut down, and a shirt that she tucked in the pants tops to show off her breasts.

She had only one small carpet bag.

"Everything I own in the whole world," she said. "I'm just a poor girl trying to make my way in life."

"By dancing and whoring," Spur said. She tried to slap him but he caught her hand. He took her carpet bag and opened it.

"Leave my things alone!" she screeched.

Spur went through everything. He found a stack of letters with a home address, a purse with over two-hundred dollars in it in greenbacks. In the back of the purse in a partially hidden slot in the leather, he saw the edge of the bank passbook. He looked at it and at first didn't believe it.

The name on the outside was Curtis Cameron, listed was a St. Louis address. In a neat small hand were entries. The last showed a balance in the savings account of $43,478.19.

"Give me that, I earned it!"

"And stole it. Curt would never give it up without a fight."

"It's mine. I'm the widow, so I'm entitled."

"Where is your marriage certificate?"

"Left it in St. Louis."

"Or that's where you'll have one forged. I think I better keep this little passbook. It will help pay for the damage to the Shuntington Circle S ranch. I can have the money impounded by the U.S. attorney in Missouri."

She flew at him, fingernails slashing, eyes furious, feet kicking.

Spur grabbed her and dumped her on the table.

"On second thought, you better find your own way back to town. The train leaves in the morning going east. You be damn sure that you're on it!"

Spur rode back to town with the others. The woman trailed them by half a mile.

He had made sure that Rutger had not heard any of the Billy Joe story, and that he had been kept busy in town so he couldn't come with them to the ranch.

The sheriff left one of the men in the barn to guard the bodies. There would be a funeral tomorrow at the ranch.

As the small group approached Laramie, Spur saw that the two companies of cavalry were still in place. Their tents were aligned as if they had been positioned by a surveyor. Half the men were taking horse drills.

As Spur rode up the company street, Major O'Reilly came to meet him.

"Sir, the troops can be ready for your inspection in five minutes if you still desire it."

"I do, sir. It is the least I can do for the service your troops performed today. I wish to commend them. How is your wounded man."

"He was not seriously hurt. His heavy cartridge belt saved his life, I'd say. The bullet was half spent by the time it penetrated the belt."

"I'd like to present that trooper with a wound medal."

"Of course sir. We have it ready."

Fifteen minutes later the eighty troopers and officers were drawn up in a formal parade formation and rode past Spur McCoy in review.

There was no band, but a bugler blew a "To the Colors" call, and the parade ended.

Spur presented the medal to the trooper who was somewhat embarrassed.

"Without your good body to accept the bullet

from the rebels, your fellow troopers would not have been permitted to fire at the raiders." Spur said. "I'm afraid even with our concentration of gunfire at the entrance to town, the raiders would have overwhelmed us and your burial detail would have had many civilians, both women and children to care for. Private Windlawn, the United States Army congratulates you!"

Spur saluted the private who smartly returned the gesture and positioned himself beside Spur and the Major as they trooped the front of the formation and then the ceremony was over.

Spur turned to the Fort Commander. "Major O'Reilly, I'll have a letter ready for your report on this action before I leave town. Again, I thank you for your help."

Back in town, it was near dark. Laramie looked almost back to normal. The boards were all down from the stores. The streets were filled with people. Some looked at the bullet holes in the buildings. A glazier was busy putting in four new windows that had been shot out.

The hardware man set up a table to accept any cartridges that the volunteers wanted to turn in.

The five walking wounded raiders were hustled into jail before the people could do them any real harm.

One more of the wounded had died. Three would be bedfast for at least two weeks, perhaps longer.

The sheriff talked to the district attorney who had filed charges of attempted murder against each of the eight men. The sheriff signed the complaints, but deleted the paperwork against Billy Joe. Spur put Billy Joe in a jail cell by himself for his own protection.

Rutger caught up with Spur as he came out of the sheriff's office.

"You found my parents?"

"We think so. You'll have to identify them tomorrow. I think it's better to have a burial on the ranch."

Rutger turned away, covered his face with both hands. He sobbed for a moment, then wiped away tears. ";I figured it had to be, but knowing for sure this way is a . . . a shock. I better go and tell Priscilla."

"I'll make the arrangements for tomorrow, preacher, flowers, everything."

"Thanks."

Spur didn't feel like eating. At the hotel, he had a bathtub brought to his room with three buckets of boiling water and one of cold. For an hour he soaked the suds and the tension away from his stiff and sore body. His thigh wound was healing well. His left shoulder was still hurting.

He had two stiff drinks of whiskey and crawled into bed, but not before he pushed a chair under the door and slid the dresser in front of the window. He didn't want anything to disturb a good night's sleep.

15

The next morning Spur worked at cleaning up the Shuntington case. He rode out to the ranch with Rutger and ten quickly hired cowboys.

The preacher came with them and a simple, private ceremony took place on a slight rise under a gnarled, twisted cottonwood. Priscilla came out by buggy with Amy Young for the service, then both went back to town.

Priscilla said she wasn't quite ready to stay at the ranch where there was so much of her mother still evident. It would take some time.

Rutger dug into the business of the ranch. The outlaws had not destroyed everything. They had figured on coming back and perhaps burning it when they left, he decided.

He appointed one newly hired man as cook, and had him inventory the root cellar, the pantry and the store room. Then sent him to town with two-hundred dollars and a wagon to stock up on food and supplies.

Next he rode out on the range to get a good picture of the stock, where they were, how many were there, what they could do with a roundup and a dozen other pieces of information he needed.

Spur rode along with him to the near range and

checked the stock, then decided the ranch was in good hands.

"Be sure to consult with the lawyer to find out how you get the grant deed returned to your name, and any other legal problems that Cameron caused. Then you'll be in the clear."

Rutger shook his hand.

"Thanks, McCoy. Next time you're in this area, be sure to stop by for a drink and a steak so thick not even you could eat it all."

Back in town, Spur checked with the sheriff. Spur wrote out a statement for the court and had it notarized. The eight men would be charged with several felonies. Conviction was almost certain.

"Both Billy Joe and that woman Lucia got on the morning train headed east," Sheriff Dryer said. "I figure that we just about have the Shuntington case all wrapped."

"Not quite," Spur said. He tossed the bank saving passbook on the sheriff's desk.

"What about your costs of extra deputies and the cost of the assault on the town, medical care for the injured, board and room, and court costs. I'd suggest you ask the circuit court judge to establish a fair price for all of this, as well as an assessment from Rutger Shuntington about the losses caused to the ranch, and at least a ten-thousand dollar fee for the wrongful death for each his mother and father.

"When the final figure has been determined by the court, this account in St. Louis should be attached by the federal court and the money sent here for payment."

Sheriff Dryer laughed, a belly whopper that shook the small office. "Damn, but you think of everything. How did you get the little passbook?"

Spur told him and the Sheriff snorted. "Not exactly a legal search of a private citizen, but who cares. It's going to work out all to the good."

Spur left his final report with the sheriff, then wrote out a letter commending Major Patrick O'Reilly and his Pony Soldiers and had it delivered to the major at the fort.

His last duty was a telegram to General Wilton D. Halleck, his boss in Washington D.C. He gave a run down on the solution to the problem, and that he was evaluating his priorities. He would be in touch with his St. Louis office and Fleur Leon.

By that time it was slightly after midday and Spur stopped in the hotel dining room for a meal. He was halfway through a trio of center cut pork chops and mashed potatoes and gravy and two kinds of vegetables, when someone slid into the chair across from him.

Priscilla watched him, her face sober, her eyes red rimmed. She wore a plain dress and had not even tried to make her hair look pretty. At least she had changed from the black dress she wore at the grave-side service at the ranch.

"Hello, Mr. McCoy. Do you mind if I sit here a minute. I just want to see a friendly face for a moment."

He stood and she motioned him down.

"My pleasure, Miss Shuntington. Do you wish something to eat? A cup of coffee?"

She shook her head.

He finished the pork chops and then pushed his plate away. The lady obviously had something on her mind.

"Could we walk for a spell?"

He said they could and took her out the side door and along a side street, the shortest way to the open country beyond town and the pleasant Laramie river.

Only then did she reach for his arm and hold it tightly.

"Do you mind, Spur. It really helps me."

"I'm honored."

They had crossed the tracks and soon came to the banks of the Laramie.

It's always seemed to me like the river runs the wrong way," Priscilla said. "I think of north as being up and south as down, and when water runs north . . .''

She bent, picked up a stone and threw it in the river. It was an unschooled woman's throw, herky-jerky.

Spur found a stone and made it skip across the water, bouncing six times before it ran out of forward motion and sank into the water.

"I like that," she said smiling up at him like a school girl. "Let's sit down in the grass and throw stones.''

He found a place that was green and soft and helped her sit down. Her skirt made a circle around her.

"I'm basic and childlike today," she said slowly. "I've seen death, the deaths of my two best friends in the whole world. Now I have to put myself and my life back together again. I hope you can be patient and help me. I've decided that I have three days to do the job.

"Then I must go back to the ranch, take over for a while and run the house until I can find a competent housekeeper. I still want to go back to school. I know my father never believed it, but I think women should be just as well educated as men. We're just as smart, and in Wyoming we can vote and hold office. Maybe I'll be governor some day!"

She looked over at him as he threw another rock. "Only five skips, you're slipping. Can you help me reconstruct my life during the next three days, Mr. McCoy?"

"Will it be difficult for me?"

She smiled and touched his shoulder. "Not at all.

You'll take me shopping, and we'll read some books, and maybe go to church, and have a picnic and some long talks. Oh, Rutger gave me a thousand dollars and I put it in the bank, so there's no problem about money."

"I wasn't worried about money."

"Can you?"

"I hope so. I sent a telegram to Washington and St. Louis. I might get word about a new assignment any time."

"I'll risk it if you will."

"Fine. Done."

"Kiss my cheek to seal the arrangement." He did and he felt her stir.

"Tell me about your mother. Talk it out, don't try to hold anything inside. If you can talk about something like death, it's easier to deal with all the smaller problems."

She lay back in the grass and Spur felt she was totally unaware of how tempting she made herself. She was a little girl again talking about her memories of her mother. She rolled over and propped her chin on her hand as she talked. All the good times, the time she was sick, then going away to school in Denver.

Before they knew it, the shadows of the river trees swept over them and Spur stood.

"It's getting late, we should start back."

"Yes, hold my hand. I feel better already. Tonight let's have dinner in that little cafe down the street, the one run by that funny little Chinese man. Then up in my room we can play dominoes. Do you know how to play?"

He knew how to play. Dinner was pleasant. Upstairs she made him wait in his room while she changed. When he came in she wore a thin cotton blouse she said was cooler. For a moment he wondered if she were trying to seduce him, but she was little girl innocent again.

She seemed not to think about romantic things or situations. Once she bent over him to whisper a funny story and her blouse swung outward showing the sides of her breasts but she didn't notice.

Spur made no move toward her. They played four games of dominoes to five-hundred, and she won two. She stood up, looked at the wind-up clock she had on the dresser.

"Goodness, it's late, after nine-thirty. We better get to bed." She held open the door. "I'll see you for breakfast promptly at nine. Then we're going to go riding down along the river. You promised me. And I'll even show you that I can use that big .44 of yours."

She held out her cheek to be kissed and he pecked her and hurried to his room. It had been an interesting afternoon and evening. He went over most of it again and no where could he find any hidden motives or any sly purpose in her actions. She was being friendly, simple, open. Indeed, it did seem like she was trying to heal the wound of the loss of her parents with a true friend.

The next morning, Spur was up long before nine o'clock. He went to the hardware store and bought a skillet, some fishing gear, some coffee and sugar and a packet of salt. At the bakery he had them make up four big sandwiches for him and then he hurried back to the hotel in time to take Priscilla to breakfast.

Later they rode upstream, south from Laramie, past the fort and toward the Colorado territory line. She was an excellent rider. Priscilla picked out her own horse at the livery and knew how to saddle the smallish mare. She wore a divided skirt and rode astride.

After an hour's ride Spur pulled them into an open area by the stream and stopped.

"Fishing time," he said. "There should be some trout in the river. We need some for our dinner. Can you fish, too?

She could.

He had fishing line and hooks, they dug for worms and cut poles from the brush. Priscilla caught the first one, a scrappy ten-incher, and Spur got a twelve-inch trout soon after that. They caught two more, then Spur cleaned the trout and built a small cooking fire.

He cut the heads and tails off and cooked the trout flat over the fire, being careful not to overcook them. With salt and the sandwiches and water from the big canteen they had their noon time meal.

They hadn't seen a soul since they passed the fort. The food was delicious, the trout boned out easily, and they ate until they were full.

"This is so wonderful I don't want it ever to change!" She fell back in a patch of daisies and smiled at him. "Isn't this delightful, Spur McCoy?"

"Yes, relaxing, calming, refreshing. But it's not all there is to life."

"Now you are a philosopher. Spur McCoy, if you had one thing you wanted in all the world, what would it be?"

"I have it now. I have a job I enjoy, a work that helps people, that solves crimes, that puts killers behind bars or in Boot Hill. I'm satisfied with that. What would you want?"

She smiled. "First to finish school, and learn so much about just everything. Then I want to find a wonderful man and get married and have four delightful children I can raise to be senators and governors and maybe even President of the United States. I have high goals."

She sat up and moved closer to him. "There is one more thing I want and I've been worried about it. Ever since Elliot Parker forced me that day. . . ."

She looked away. Then she stared deliberately at
Spur, caught his hand and pushed it inside her loose
blouse.

"Spur, please, *please* show me what it's like to
make love with a man you love and respect. Please,
Spur, right now. It's the one last thing I need to
experience so I can accept all that's happened to me
in the last few days. Then I'll be able to help Rutger
get the ranch moving again, and then go back to
school in Denver and finish my education."

Spur felt his hand on her bare breasts. She had on
nothing under the blouse. Slowly his hand curled
around a breast and he felt it throbbing. Her nipple
burned his palm.

Slowly she lifted up and kissed his lips. For a
moment he didn't move. Then she kissed him again
and her lips opened and her tongue licked his lips
until they parted.

Her tongue darted inside his mouth exploring.
She shivered and then her hand reached for his
crotch and rubbed tenderly. His erection began and
she found it and massaged it with great care.

He eased away from her lips.

"Priscilla, we can't. It's not right. I'll be going
away. It's just not right."

"Spur McCoy, I'm the one asking. I know I can't
seduce you, but I would if I knew how. *I need you to
make love to me.* It's simple. I want you. I need to
know love at its best, when it's tender and thoughtful and slow and loving!"

She watched him. He hadn't moved his hand. It
rubbed her breasts gently. Her hand covered his
growing erection.

"Besides, I owe you the favor. You kept me from
being killed by the raiders. You saved our ranch and
drove off the killers. I need to give you something.
It will make me feel so much better."

Her hands slipped the buttons loose from her

blouse and she slid it off her shoulders.

Her breasts were larger than he had guessed, perfect mounds topped with wide pink areolas and blood red nipples.

"Please?" she pleaded.

"My god but you are beautiful!" he said, his voice catching.

She kissed him again, their tongues twining. Priscilla gave little moans and yelps of joy as she knew he was going to show her what true loving felt like.

When the long kiss ended, she caught his head and brought it down to her breasts.

"No one has ever kissed my breasts, Spur. Would you?"

He took a deep breath and caught the creamy white orbs, kissing each tenderly, working around them in circles that moved upward until he reached her pulsating nipples. When he kissed her second one, Priscilla moaned and then yelped. Her whole body went rigid for a moment and she clutched at him as a sharp series of spasms shook her.

Her hips pounded toward his. She rolled toward him and pumped her hips against his erection at least a dozen times before the spasms receded and she sighed and barely opened her eyes.

"Oh, god but that was marvelous! So wonderful. What is it going to be like when you push inside me?"

He kissed her and took off his shirt. She toyed with the black hair on his chest.

"Do all men have hair on their chests?"

"No. But some much more than this." Spur let her unbuckle his belt and open his pants, then he pulled them off with his short underwear and turned toward her.

"Oh my!" she said, her eyes wide. She glanced at him quickly. "He's so big. A friend at school said some are bigger than others."

Spur chuckled. "Girls talk about such things?"

"Only sometimes when we're lonely and feeling kind of wild."

She reached out, then her hand came back. "May I?"

"You better," he said smiling.

She knelt in front of him where he lay naked in the grass and touched and pulled and examined his genitals.

"I've never had a chance to look at. . . ." she ducked her head. "Hope you don't mind."

"I like it," Spur said, his hands caressing her hanging, swinging breasts.

"I like you touching me, too." A moment later she sat back, satisfied. She looked up at him. "Would you take the rest of my clothes off . . . gently?"

"If you want me to."

He removed her skirt, then a split petticoat, and when he touched her tight, form fitting drawers that buttoned to the knee and were full of tiny satin bows, she stopped him.

"Maybe that's enough for today," he said.

"Oh, no, it's just that for so long I've thought that I'd never let a man . . . you know . . . take off my clothes until I was married."

"No rush," Spur said stroking her breasts.

"Oh, that feels so marvelous." She looked at him. "Will it feel that good when you go . . . you know, when you push it inside me?"

"I've been told it's a dozen times better than anything else. That the thrusting is pure heaven."

She sighed, kissed him again, then bent and kissed his belly near his penis and put her hands on the buttons holding her drawers on.

A few moments later she pulled the drawers down and off her feet.

Her dark muff was thick and luxuriant. At once

she rolled on top of him. He kissed her again, then his hand found its way between them and caressed the triangle of dark hair.

Slowly she spread her legs and his hand found her heartland that was already wet. He touched her clit and she roared into another climax, bounding and humping at him where she lay on top of him.

Beads of perspiration collected on her forehead and she closed her eyes as the tremors shimmered and slanted through her delightful young body.

When it was over she nodded at him.

"Now, Spur McCoy, before I lose my nerve again. I want you to come inside me, right now!"

He rolled over in the grass, pushing her on the bottom. Gently he spread her legs and lifted her knees and went between them. She looked down at his stiff penis, then closed her eyes. He found her slot and slowly edged in. She yelped and he thrust harder, then he was past the membrane and sliding smoothly and well lubricated deep into her.

"Oh my god!" Priscilla whispered. "Never in the world have I felt anything so . . . so wonderful! It's magic, it's sailing over the moon! I felt nothing like this before, the first time."

Spur slid almost out and drove back in and she squealed in rapture and raced to another climax. She locked her arms around his neck and he could see the sweat on her forehead.

Ten times she climaxed as he worked her along. Then Spur could hold back no longer and he thrust forward hard half a dozen times and fired his jolts of jism into her waiting vessel.

Priscilla climaxed again as he was grunting and yelping and sounding like a steam engine. They collapsed together and held each other tightly until they could breathe normally.

She shifted and he lifted away, but she held him. "Don't go, not yet. I want to remember this for as long as I live."

"You will," he said. "But never tell your husband, or any other living soul. This was part of your healing, part of growing up, and it's nobody's business but ours. Promise?"

She nodded. He kissed her, then lifted out of her and sat on the grass.

They both looked at the water.

"Skinny dipping?" Spur said and they raced for the river. It was mountain snow fed from the Colorado snow pack, and they stepped in only to screech in surprise. They splashed each other a little but quickly came out of the calf deep water to lay on the grass in the sun to get warm.

Again, Priscilla talked. She told Spur about her childhood, and growing up. How good it had been on the ranch. Her parents were special people, kind and thoughtful, generous with the hands, keeping on many year round when there was a little or no work for them to do to earn their wages.

They had the smallest turnover in cowboys of any ranch in the territory.

At last they kissed once more, then dressed and put away the cooking things and got ready to ride. It was after three in the afternoon.

"Where did the time go?" Priscilla asked. She looked at Spur and they both giggled.

"Time goes fast when you're enjoying yourself, and making love with someone you love," Spur said. He did love her, perhaps just for the day, but it was real and solid even though not lasting.

They rode back to town. She said she was going to have a long hot bath and would be ready for supper at eight. Spur checked with the Sheriff, then the telegraph office. The afternoon train came through bringing in half a dozen new people, but no problems.

When he got to the telegraph office, the operator looked up and nodded.

"Tried to find you this noon, Mr. McCoy. I have two wires for you. Must be important."

Spur took the two envelopes and walked back to the hotel.

He wasn't going to open them yet. Both had to be about a new assignment. He'd get to it, eventually. First he was going to have a long, luxurious, supper with a beautiful girl. Then they would play dominoes until ten o'clock.

After that he would take a look at the telegrams. It was at times like this that Spur McCoy wondered if he had been in the field too long. Now and then he had a touch of resentment when a new assignment came in. Once in a great while, he wished he could just settle down and stay in one place for a whole six months, maybe even a year!

He could make friends, maybe even get married and have a son or two. Oh, and at least one little girl! That would restrict the kind of assignments he could take.

Spur shook his head. What in hell was he thinking about? He was a field man. He had the whole western half of the U.S. as his territory. And he had covered almost all of it from time to time.

An itch began to grow in the back of his mind. Where would he be going next? The Pacific Coast maybe. Washington State? Or way up in Montana near the Canadian border? Maybe Apache country down in New Mexico or Arizona?

Spur pushed down the itch, walked into the first bar he passed and ordered a cold bottle of beer.

He looked at the two envelopes. When the beer was drained, he tore open one of the telegrams and began to read.

"CONGRATULATIONS ON YOUR WRAP-

PING UP THE SHUNTINGTON RANCH TAKE-
OVER CASE. WE HAVE A NEW PROBLEM. IT
SEEMS THAT THERE IS A SERIOUS
SITUATION THAT YOU NEED TO LOOK INTO
AS SOON AS POSSIBLE IT'S IN. . . .''

Spur McCoy pushed the telegram back in his
pocket unread. So it was a new assignment. He
would read it later tonight, after he had kissed a
pretty girl good night and walked back to his room.

Nothing was going to spoil his last night in
Laramie. He owed the lady that much. That much
and a little bit more.

Spur McCoy hurried over to the Medicine Bow
Hotel. The lady had not said that he couldn't help
her take her bath. There might be a good chance, if
he hurried before she was through.

There was a new spring in Spur McCoy's step as
he marched up the hotel stairs toward the third
floor. Yes, he thought, there was an extremely good
chance that he could hire on to wash a back. Who
knows, maybe even a front!

Spur McCoy grinned as he knocked on Priscilla's
door. Yeah, he was a field man!